THE TOWN CATS

AND OTHER TALES

THE TOWN CATS

AND OTHER TALES

Lloyd Alexander

Illustrated by Laszlo Kubinyi

A YEARLING BOOK

Published by
Dell Publishing Co., Inc.
1 Dag Hammarskjold Plaza
New York, New York 10017

Yearling ® TM 913705, Dell Publishing Co., Inc.

ISBN: 0–440–48989–X

Reprinted by arrangement with E. P. Dutton, a division of
Elsevier-Dutton Publishing Co., Inc.

Printed in the United States of America

First Yearling printing—March 1981

CW

*For cat-keepers, and others
wise enough to laugh at themselves*

Contents

THE TOWN CATS

AND OTHER TALES

The Town Cats

VALDORO was the smallest town in the farthest corner of the Kingdom of Mondragone. Its people being honest, sensible, and prudent, it boasted no great men of state, scholarship, or military glory. The town council once had given thought to raising a statue of its most distinguished citizen; but, as no accord could be reached on whom this might be, or if indeed there was one, the pedestal in the square stood empty. Valdoro, thus, for many years went happily unknown, unnoticed, and ignored.

One day, however, Ser Basilio, the mayor, received a document from the Directorate of Provincial Affairs. It stated that a Deputy Provincial Commissioner, one Ser Malocchio, would arrive that very afternoon to obtain permanent residence and to supervise all local activities. Henceforth, following the recommendations of the said Deputy Provisional Commissioner, the inhabitants of Valdoro would share the blessings and benefits enjoyed by their fellow subjects throughout the realm.

"He'll skin us alive with taxes!" cried the cloth merchant, after Basilio had read the pronouncement to

13

all the townsfolk gathered in the square. "Better a visit from the seven-year itch!"

"He'll send all our lads into the army!" wailed the barber's daughter.

"He'll set lawyers, clerks, and notaries among us," the baker cried. "Rather a dozen pickpockets than one of them!"

So, the folk of Valdoro, and Ser Basilio no less than anyone, bemoaned this evil day, sure that never again would they call their lives their own.

Now, there was in Valdoro a certain mackerel-striped cat, Pescato by name. Long-tailed, long-legged, with jaunty tufts of fur at the tips of his ears, this Pescato was known to all as the boldest rascal ever on four paws. Glib enough to wheedle his way into any house he chose, he liked better the streets and alleys. Days, he sunned himself on the pedestal; nights, he prowled the byways or perched on a chimney pot, where he sang melodiously until dawn. He was sleek as an otter, for never in his life had he missed a meal. As the folk of Valdoro kept many cats, most of them related to him one way or another, he could always accept hospitality from his kindred. He preferred, however, living by his wits; to Pescato, a neatly swindled chicken wing tasted sweeter than a whole fowl without the sauce of a clever venture.

That morning, while Ser Basilio and the townsfolk wept and wailed, tore their hair, and gnashed their teeth at the disaster soon to overtake them, Pescato sat on the steps of the town hall, calmly observing these doings. At last, he got up, unfurled his tail, stretched himself, and went to the mayor, saying:

"My dear friend Basilio, how foolish to let a trifle spoil such a pleasant day."

"Trifle?" cried Basilio, looking ready to fall to the ground from sheer dismay. "You'll call it a trifle when this Malocchio sets about his poking and prying? Ah, misery of miseries! I can feel those blessings and benefits already, like a hot mustard plaster on my back!"

"Every cat's a kingdom in himself," replied Pescato, "and we rule ourselves better than anyone can rule for us. Alas, the same can't be said for you human creatures."

"Do you think you'll escape?" retorted Basilio. "No, no, my fine fellow. You'll be pinched and squeezed along with the rest of us; and so, too, your kittens, your nephews, nieces, and cousins, and every cat in Valdoro. Will you have table scraps when we can't afford crust or crumb on our tables? If it's to be lean pickings for us, then for you no pickings at all."

"A cat can always make a living in the world," replied Pescato. "However, as you tell it, I recognize certain inconveniences." Then, after a few moments of thought, Pescato added:

"Come, cheer up. This is a simple matter, easily set right."

"So you say," returned Basilio, casting a doubting eye on Pescato, since the mayor had more than once been on the wrong end of the cat's enterprises. As he listened to Pescato's plan, he frowned, shook his head, and declared this would be an impossible endeavor. He soon realized, however, there was no hope otherwise; and admitted the cat's scheme to be better than his own, which was none whatever. So, at last he agreed that all should be done according to Pescato's instruction.

"Very well," said Pescato. "Now, Basilio, fetch me your sash, your ermine cloak and cap, and your chain of office."

The mayor did as the cat required of him, being assured by Pescato that all this regalia would be returned before the day ended.

"Believe me," Pescato said, "I have no desire to be mayor a moment longer than need be. Therefore, the sooner we get about our business, the sooner you shall be once again in office."

So saying, Pescato wrapped the sash around his middle, hung the chain from his neck, and draped the cloak over his shoulders. Thus garbed, and leaving Basilio to certain other duties, Pescato cocked the hat on his head and set off for the bridge he knew Ser Malocchio would be obliged to cross.

There he patiently waited until he glimpsed four horses drawing a gilded coach. As the vehicle clattered over the bridge, Pescato stepped forward and raised a paw. As the coachman, astonished at the sight, hastily pulled up, the occupant, who was none other than Ser Malocchio himself, thrust his bewigged head out the window and stared in both amazement and indignation.

"What mockery is this?" he cried. Ser Malocchio was a lean-faced, lantern-jawed fellow with a high-ridged nose and a mouth that snapped open and shut like a cash box. His cheeks turned as crimson as the jacket of his uniform, and he shook his fist at Pescato:

"A cat! Tricked out in robes and chains! An insult! A damnable impertinence! Out of my way, beast. We shall

16

soon see who put you up to this. Make sport of a royal officer? That will prove a costly game."

In spite of this outburst, Pescato doffed his hat, swept a deep and graceful bow, and courteously replied:

"Excellency, allow me humbly to assure you: Things are not as you might suppose. Mock you? On the contrary, I am here in my official capacity to welcome you to Valdoro, and to convey the most respectful greetings of my townspeople."

"A cat, mayor of a town?" returned Malocchio, still scowling, but a little softened, nevertheless, by Pescato's deference. "You have strange customs in this part of the country."

"Your Honor," answered Pescato, "let me only say again: All is not what it may seem, as I shall presently explain to you. Meantime, forgive me if I am unable to express fully the sensations that stir my heart at your arrival, and the knowledge that our modest village has been deemed worthy of your attention. I could not begin to describe our feelings at the prospect of all the blessings and benefits you must have in store for us; indeed, they are truly unspeakable."

"Intelligent creature!" exclaimed Malocchio, more and more kindly disposed toward Pescato. Never before had his presence offered the occasion for such agreeable words, and he was delighted to accept such a welcome even from a cat. "Small wonder you are mayor of this town; for I perceive in you rare qualities of statesmanship, and a keen appreciation of the nature of civic administration."

"May I say in all modesty," answered Pescato, "no one appreciates it more than I."

17

"My dear sir," cried Malocchio, "what pleasure it is to hear that. Worthy colleague, do me the honor of joining me in my coach."

"Gladly, Your Worshipful Excellence," said Pescato, climbing in beside him and ordering the coachman to drive in the direction of the town hall. "I am eager and impatient to learn of your plans for Valdoro, and trust you will reveal them to me without delay. In addition, I have certain suggestions of my own which I earnestly hope you will allow me to offer you."

"Initiative on the part of His Majesty's subjects is always highly esteemed," replied Malocchio, "depending, of course, on the degree to which it enhances His Majesty's treasury."

"And perhaps your own, as well?" said Pescato, with a wink. "For it seems to me, worthy Ser Malocchio, that your efforts on behalf of our town should be generously, though discreetly, compensated."

"How clearly statesmen understand each other," replied Malocchio, grinning with all his teeth. "It gratifies me to anticipate that we shall conjoin to our mutual advantage."

"Like two rogues at a town fair," said Pescato, adding quickly, "an old country expression we use in this corner of the world. Now, to the business at hand. First, I suggest and beseech you to consider establishing a garrison of militia, constabulary, and watchmen. Naturally, for this luxury, our citizens would be overjoyed to pay their wages—through your good offices, of course, leaving the matter of disbursement entirely in your hands."

"Exactly the manner in which it should be done,"

returned Malocchio. "Nothing is more efficacious and economical, and saves burdensome record-keeping."

"You should also know," Pescato went on, "that I am hardly able to restrain the men of our town, especially the lame, the halt, and the blind, from their eagerness not to serve in one of the royal regiments. So I suggest that their heroic impulses be expressed through payment of a fee; and so that all may be just and equitable, the greater their ardor, the larger the sum."

"What nicety!" cried Malocchio. "What a delicate discernment!"

"Your official residence is not quite prepared," continued Pescato. "Until it is, I trust you will do me the honor of being my guest. The elegance of my establishment, if I myself dare say so, is no less than you deserve. I assure you I live exactly as I choose; which, in my opinion, is rather well indeed."

"I sense, dear colleague, that you are one who enjoys the finer things of life," said Malocchio. "I should not dream of denying you the pleasure of sharing them with me."

The coach by now had only passed through the outskirts of the town when the coachman suddenly reined up. Vexed at the delay, Malocchio peered out to discover the cause. Stammering, he fell back onto his seat.

In the middle of the street, crouching on all fours, naked as radishes, were Taddeo the barber and Mascolo the butcher. Hissing, spitting, yelling in frenzy, they scuttled back and forth, circling, darting to one side then the other. Next instant, Taddeo shot out his hand and fetched Mascolo a smack on the head; at the same time, Mascolo fetched Taddeo a cuff on the ear. In a trice, barber and butcher went at it hammer and tongs, rolling over the cobbles, grappling, kicking, and miauling at the top of their voices.

"Can I believe my eyes?" cried Malocchio. "Who, sir, are they? Your village idiots?"

"Bobtail and Whitepaw?" replied Pescato. "They mean each other no harm. Those two cats are forever squabbling."

"Cats?" exclaimed Malocchio. "Cats, you say? Those? But—but you, yourself—"

Pescato shook his head and raised a paw to his lips. "There are, dear friend, certain, shall I say, local conditions. But they are better discussed in private."

Ser Malocchio had managed to accommodate himself to the notion of dealing with a cat as mayor; but now, having heard two unquestionable men referred to as cats, all began turning topsy-turvy in his head. However, before he could ask further, the coach rattled into the square and, at Pescato's command, drew up in front of the town hall. Pescato beckoned for the bewildered functionary to descend and follow him into the building. And if Ser Malocchio had been taken aback at the sight of the barber and butcher, he gaped all the more at what he presently observed.

For here were some dozen townsfolk scattered throughout the square, perched on barrels, curled on steps, or drowsing on window ledges. In Taddeo's barber shop, one of Pescato's cousins, garbed in a white apron, had mounted a high stool and was busy snipping away at the whiskers of one of Pescato's nephews. In

21

the tailor shop, as one cat measured another for a waist-coat, his assistant, a young orange-and-white cat, un-rolled a bolt of cloth, while the human tailor sat cross-legged in a corner, toying with a spool of thread. By the fish market, the fishwife scurried after her three little ones to snatch them up and lick their ears. The greengrocer sped past on all fours, in hot pursuit of a mouse. From the upper windows of the houses, cats and kittens in dust caps and ribbons peered down and waved their paws in welcome.

"What manner of town is this?" babbled Malocchio, following Pescato into the mayor's chambers. There, Malocchio clapped hands to his head; for, stretched full length on the council table, was Ser Basilio.

"Naughty creature," Pescato chided, shaking a finger at the mayor. "How often have I told you never to sleep on official papers!"

In response, Basilio rolled over on his back, waving hands and feet in the air. Pescato, clicking his tongue in fond reproach, tickled the mayor under the chin.

"Good fellow," said Pescato, while Basilio purred and wriggled with delight. "But enough now. Off you go! Behave yourself and you'll have a fine bit of mackerel for your supper."

The mayor sprang from the table and loped out the door, while Malocchio's jaws snapped open and shut as though he were trying vainly to disgorge the words stuck like so many fishbones in his gullet.

"You were about to say that I spoil him?" remarked Pescato. "Yes, no doubt I do. But we must indulge our pets for the sake of the pleasure they give us. Now, a

22

moment of pleasure for ourselves before considering our affairs," he continued, settling himself in the mayor's high-backed chair. Taking up a little silver bell, he rang it briskly.

"Ah—ah, Honorable Mayor, colleague—" Malocchio at last was able to stammer, squirming uneasily on the seat Pescato had indicated. "Before all else, you must explain to me—"

That moment, Pescato's uncle, a stately gray cat with a steward's key hanging from his neck, came bearing a tray of food and a goblet of wine. Bowing solemnly, he presented this refreshment to Malocchio, who gratefully seized the goblet in trembling hands and immediately gulped down most of its contents.

"You appear a little distracted, my dear friend," said Pescato. "The result, no doubt, of your long journey. And I quite understand you may have been somewhat unsettled by our particular condition. I assure you, we no longer consider it in the least way disturbing. We go about our business as usual, as you have seen for yourself."

"As usual?" cried Malocchio. "Great merciful heavens, whatever has befallen you?"

"The situation you may have noticed," said Pescato, "has come upon us quite recently. I might even say with a degree of suddenness." Here, Pescato made a show of reluctance to speak further; but, after some hesitation, he continued:

"Needless to say, I rely on your absolute discretion. If so much as a whisper should reach the Provincial Directorate as to the cause of our transformation—you

can foresee the consequences. No one would ever set foot in Valdoro, or have anything whatever to do with us."

"What are you hiding?" burst out Malocchio. "An epidemic? An infestation? Has some horrible disease made your cats look like people, and your people cats?"

"Disease?" replied Pescato. "Indeed, sir, never have I felt better in my life. I confess it was discomfiting at first. But one quickly grows accustomed, and even comes to enjoy it. As you will."

"I?" shouted Malocchio, springing to his feet. "I? What are you telling me?"

"Yes, you too, since you shall be living among us," replied Pescato. "After the peculiar occurrence, we made every effort to determine the cause. We concluded it was the wine."

"Wine?" choked Malocchio, spewing out the last mouthful he had taken, and flinging away the goblet.

"Calm yourself," said Pescato. "We soon understood it was not our wine, since not all of us drink it. And so we judged it must be the food."

"Food?" cried Malocchio, sweeping aside the tray of refreshments. "Poison!"

"Be at ease," Pescato assured him. "Eat your fill. It was not the food, nor the water. We examined both and found no fault with either."

Malocchio heaved a sigh of relief. But Pescato continued:

"No, none of these things. In the firm opinion of the town physician, the apothecary, and all our learned individuals: beyond any doubt, it is the air."

"Air?" sputtered Malocchio. "Did you say air?"

"The very air you are breathing at this instant," said Pescato.

Hearing this, Malocchio gave a shriek of horror, emptied his lungs in a great gust, clapped one hand over his mouth and the other over his nose. Stifling his gasps, terrified to draw so much as another breath, he dashed from the chamber. While his face turned at first red, then lavender, then purple for want of air, he threw himself into the coach, buried his head under the seat cushions, and went galloping out of town, never stopping and scarcely breathing until he reached the capital.

Never again was Valdoro troubled with any Provincial Commissioners. Nor did Ser Malocchio reveal what he had seen, lest his superiors think him altogether out of his wits. Instead, he claimed that a terrible pestilence had stricken the town and not one human being remained. So Valdoro was removed from the maps and blotted from the archives, and a special directive was issued declaring the town had never existed in the first place. Yet, ever after, Ser Malocchio was continually scrutinizing his face in the mirror, fearful that he might at any moment sprout cat's whiskers or grow fur from his ears.

And so the folk of Valdoro happily resumed their former ways. Pescato was proclaimed Town Cat; and the mayor and the council unanimously voted to raise a bronze figure of him. Pescato, however, declined this honor, seeing no reason to give up his comfortable spot on the pedestal for the sake of a mere statue.

The Cat-King's Daughter

PRINCESS ELENA of Ventadorn loved Raimond, Count of Albiclair. However, as much as the two young people had set their hearts on marrying, so King Hugo, father of Elena, had set his against it.

"That lute plucker?" cried Hugo. "That verse scribbler? He should be out hunting, or carousing; or invading the next province, like any self-respecting nobleman. Worse yet, his estates are unspeakably small and his fortune intolerably smaller. In short, the fellow's worthless."

"That's your opinion," said Elena. "Not mine."

"Indeed it is," replied Hugo. "And whose judgment better than the King's?"

"You say that about everything," declared Elena. "Because pickled herrings happen to give you colic, you've forbidden them to all your subjects. Because holidays bore you, the kingdom has none. You can't abide cats, so you've made it a crime to keep one, to feed one, or even to shelter a kitten."

"So it should be," retorted the King. "Cats! Impudent beasts! They won't fetch or carry. They wave their tails

27

in your face. They stare at you bold as brass, then stick out their tongues and go to washing themselves."

"I call that clean," said Elena, "hardly criminal."

"Worse than criminal, it's disrespectful," snapped the King. "Disobedient and insolent, like headstrong girls who don't take no for an answer."

So, the more Elena urged his consent to marry Raimond, the more stubbornly the King refused. Instead, he sent word for other suitors properly—and profitably—qualified to present themselves at court; and he locked Princess Elena in her chambers, there to receive them and choose one to be her husband.

Princess Elena matched her father in strength of will; and no sooner was the door bolted after her than she determined to escape and make her way to Raimond as quickly as she could. But her chambers in the North Tower of the palace were too high for her to jump from the casement. Since King Hugo disliked ivy, none grew along the steep walls; and, without a handhold, the stones were too smooth for her to clamber down. Though she pulled the sheets and coverlets from her bed and knotted them together, this makeshift ladder barely reached halfway to the courtyard below. The more she cast about for other means, the more clearly she saw there were none. At last, she threw herself on the couch, crying in rage and frustration.

Then she heard a voice say:

"Princess, why do you weep?"

At her feet sat a tabby cat, honey-colored with dark stripes, thin as a mackerel, every rib showing under her bedraggled coat. Though she looked more used to alleys than palaces, she seemed quite at ease amid the soft carpets and embroidered draperies. Instead of crouching fearfully, she studied the Princess with bold curiosity through emerald eyes much the same hue as those of Elena.

"If I had satin cushions to sleep on," said the cat, "and goosedown quilts, and silken bedspreads, I wouldn't be in such a hurry to leave them."

"A cat?" exclaimed the Princess, for a moment forgetting her predicament. "But there are no cats in the palace."

"Well, there is one now," answered the cat, "and my name is Margot." She then explained how she had slipped through the palace gate that morning while the guard was changing.

"But why?" asked Elena. "You must know how my father feels about cats. And here, of all places—"

"Where better?" said Margot. "Who'd expect to find a cat under King Hugo's very nose? I was hoping for a warm cubbyhole to hide in, and a few leftovers from the kitchen. But once inside the palace, I had to dodge so many courtiers, and got so turned around in the hallways and staircases, I was glad for the first open door I came to."

"Poor creature," said Elena, venturing to stroke the cat, "you're hardly more than skin and bones."

"Thanks to your father's decree," said Margot. "Luckily, some people have better sense than to pay it any mind. Now and again, a housewife puts out some scraps or a saucer of milk. For the rest, we forage as best we can. King Hugo hasn't made life easy for a cat."

"Nor a princess," replied Elena, glad for the chance to unburden her heart by telling her troubles to Margot.

After listening attentively to the account, the cat thoughtfully preened her whiskers for several moments, then said:

"We cats won't abide doing what we're forced to do, so I understand your feelings. But I doubt very much you can be made to marry against your will. King Hugo may rant and rave; but, practically speaking, he surely won't tie you hand and foot and drag you by the hair to the wedding ceremony. A bride, kicking and screaming? Hardly flattering for a husband-to-be."

"True," Elena admitted. "But I love Raimond and want him for my husband. How shall I make my father change his mind? What if no one else claimed my hand? I'll make sure they don't! I'll paste a wart on the end of my nose, and paint myself a mustache. That should be discouraging enough."

"Princess," said the cat, "your beauty is too great to hide, no matter what you do."

"I won't eat," said Elena. "I'll starve myself."

"Be sensible," said the cat. "Your father need only wait. Your hunger will soon get the best of you."

"I'm afraid you're right," Elena agreed. "Very well, when these suitors come, I'll refuse to see them. Let them break down the door! I shan't speak a word to them. There's nothing else I can do."

"Yes, there is," said the cat. "What I have in mind might even help us cats as well as you. First, you must do as I ask now. Then, tomorrow, you must stay hidden under the couch. Be warned, however: What happens may bring you joy—or it may break your heart."

Princess Elena could not imagine herself more heartbroken than she was. And so, despite the cat's warning, she willingly agreed. As Margot instructed her, she combed and brushed the cat until the fur was as soft and glistening as her own tresses. Then she draped the cat in one of her silken scarves and tied a necklace of pearls at Margot's waist. She set a diamond bracelet as a crown on Margot's head; and adorned the cat's paws and tail with the finest rings of emeralds, rubies, and sapphires.

Next morning, King Hugo came to order his daughter to make ready for her suitors. But instead of Elena, out of sight beneath the couch, he found Margot, royally attired, comfortably stretched out amid the satin pillows.

"What's this?" roared the King. "What's this cat doing here? Scat! Scat!" He shouted for Elena, but she never stirred. Before the King thought to search the chambers, Margot glanced calmly at him and, in a voice resembling that of Elena, said:

"Father, how is it that you don't recognize your own daughter?"

At this, King Hugo stared speechless and his head began to whirl. Seeing nothing of Princess Elena in the apartments, he could only believe that she had indeed turned into a cat overnight. Then his bewilderment changed to anger and he shook a finger under Margot's nose:

"You've done it on purpose," he cried, "out of sheer stubbornness, to vex and spite me! How you managed it, I don't know. But I command you: Turn yourself back again! Immediately!"

"That," said Margot, "will be impossible."

King Hugo then declared he would summon the

Royal Physician; or, if need be, scour the kingdom for alchemists, astrologers, midwives, village wonder-workers, whoever might transform her once again into human shape.

"That will be of no use," Margot said. "As you see me now, so shall I always be."

"Wretched girl!" King Hugo cried. "Do you mean to make a fool of me? What king ever had a cat for a daughter!"

"What cat ever had a king for a father?" Margot replied.

This only enraged King Hugo the more; and he swore, cat or no, she would receive her suitors and marry the first who was willing.

And so, when the Court Chamberlain came to announce the arrival of Duke Golo de Gobino, the King tried to compose himself and put the best face he could on the matter. For Golo, while hardly the cleverest, was the richest nobleman in the kingdom, with a purse as full as his head was empty. His estates lay beside those of the King; he had a fine regiment of cavalry, excellent stables and kennels, and his marriage to Elena would be all King Hugo ever could wish.

However, when Duke Golo saw the bejeweled Margot, his self-satisfied smile vanished, and he stammered in dismay:

"The Princess? She looks rather like a cat!"

"Pay it no mind," King Hugo said. "She's not quite herself today."

"So I see," replied Golo. "Indeed, I never would have recognized her. Whatever happened?"

"Nothing," said King Hugo. "A trivial indisposition, a minor ailment."

"But, Majesty," quavered Golo, "it may be contagious. Suppose I caught it from her. If I take her for my wife, the same could happen to me."

"In your case," said Margot, "it might be an advantage."

"Come now, Golo," the King insisted, "get on with it. She'll make you a fine wife."

"One thing certain," added Margot, "you'll never be troubled with mice."

"Majesty," stammered Golo, "I came for your daughter's hand, not her paw."

"Golo!" bellowed the King. "I command you to marry her. Come back here!" But Duke Golo had already darted through the door and was making his way in all haste down the corridor.

King Hugo stormed at the cat for having lost him such a desirable son-in-law. But next came Count Bohamel de Braise, and the King once again tried to put a fair face on bad fortune. Though his estates were not as large as Golo's, Bohamel was a harsh overlord and what he lacked in land he made up in taxing his tenants; and, at this match, King Hugo would have been well satisfied.

However, when Count Bohamel saw Margot, he threw back his head and gave a rasping laugh:

"Majesty, you make sport of me. Some wives have been called cats, but no cat's been called wife. Look at her claws! They'd tear the bedsheets to ribbons. If I ever dared embrace her, she'd scratch me to the bone."

"Your claws are sharper than mine," said Margot. "Ask your tenants."

No matter how King Hugo commanded or cajoled, pleaded or threatened, Bohamel would have no part of marriage with a cat-princess.

"Your misfortune is your own, and not mine," he told the King, and strode from the chamber.

The same happened with the suitors who followed. Each, in turn, found one pretext or another:

"Good heavens, Majesty," protested the Marquis de Cabasson, shuddering. "With a wife like that, I could never invite my friends to dine. She'd never use the proper fork. And what a breach of etiquette when she drank from a saucer."

"I daresay your friends would be too deep in their cups," answered Margot, "to notice what I did with a saucer."

"A cat-wife?" sneered the Seigneur de Malcourir. "She'd dance on the rooftops with every passing tom."

"I assure you," said Margot, "my virtue's greater than yours."

By this time, word had spread through the palace that King Hugo's daughter had become a cat. The councillors and ministers gossiped, the court ladies tittered, the footmen snickered, the kitchen maids giggled; and soon all in the palace were whispering behind their hands or laughing up their sleeves.

"See what you've done!" cried the King. "Shamed me! Humiliated me!"

"How so?" asked Margot. "I'm not ashamed of being a cat. Are you ashamed of being a king?"

King Hugo threw himself down on a chair and held

his head in his hands. Not only had his daughter turned into a cat, it was now plain to him she would also turn into a spinster; and instead of a profitable marriage, there would be none at all. He began groaning miserably, blaming his daughter's stubbornness for putting him in such a plight.

That moment, the Court Chamberlain announced the suitors had departed, all but one: Count Raimond.

"How dare he come here?" exclaimed the King. "He's as pigheaded as my daughter—no, no, I don't mean that. Go fetch him, then." He turned to Margot. "Let the fellow see for himself what you've done. You've outwitted yourself this time, my girl. Marry you? One look and he'll change his tune. But at any rate, I'll have seen the last of him."

Alarmed at this, it was all Princess Elena could do to keep silent in her hiding place. She had never expected Raimond to present himself at court, knowing her father would only refuse him. Now she remembered Margot's warning. If Raimond, too, believed her a cat, indeed her heart would break. Margot, sensing her anguish, dangled her tail over the edge of the couch and waved the tip like a cautioning finger.

The Chamberlain ushered in Count Raimond. To Elena, he had never looked handsomer nor had she loved him so much; and she burned to go to him then and there. But, worse than a broken heart was not knowing the strength of his love for her. So, tormented though she was, she bravely held her tongue.

At sight of the cat, Raimond halted. He stood silent a long moment before he said to King Hugo:

"What I heard of Princess Elena I took for idle gossip. Now I see it is true."

With that, he stepped forward and bowed to Margot. Taking her paw in his hand, he said:

"Why, Princess, how well you look today. What a marvelous color your fur is. The stripes set it off to perfection. Your paws are softer than velvet. And what handsome whiskers, fine as threads of silk. You're beautiful as a cat as you were beautiful as a woman."

"What are you saying?" burst out King Hugo. "Have you gone mad? Paying court to a cat?"

"She's still my beloved as much as she's still your daughter," answered Raimond. "Do true lovers part because the hair of one goes white or the back of the other goes bent? Because the cheeks of one may wither, or the eyes of the other may dim? So long as her heart stays unchanged, so shall mine."

"Do you mean to tell me you'd marry her anyway?" cried King Hugo. "You, stand as bridegroom? And I, give her away? She'd make both of us look like fools."

"Majesty," said Raimond, "the only one who can make you look a fool is yourself. Yes. I will marry her if she will have it so. As for you, can it be that you love your daughter less than I love my intended? And yourself more than anyone else?"

At this, King Hugo began blustering and grumbling again. But, after a moment, he hung his head in shame. Finally, he said:

"My daughter is my daughter, whatever ill has befallen her; and I would have helped her least when she needed me the most. Well, Count of Albiclair, you're

37

not the son-in-law I'd have chosen; but the choice was never mine in the first place. Marry, the two of you, if that's what you want. I still don't give a fig for your lute-plucking and verse-scribbling; but I do give you my blessing."

For her part, Elena was overjoyed at these words, and more than ever assured that Raimond was her true love. Again, she was about to leave her hiding place when, to her dismay, she heard Margot reply:

"Alas, there can be no wedding. Our marriage is out of the question."

"What do you mean?" roared King Hugo, now as determined to see his daughter wed Raimond as he had been against it. "You bedeviled me to give my consent. Now you have it."

"By your own decree, cats are against the law," said Margot. "How shall Raimond keep me as a wife when it's forbidden to keep a cat?"

"Blast the decree!" retorted the King. "That's the stupidest thing I ever heard of. I made that law, so I can change it. From this day on, cats are welcome everywhere, even in my palace. In fact, I'll proclaim a new law that all my subjects must obey: Everyone must keep a cat."

"No, Majesty," answered Margot. "Only let cats freely choose their people, and people choose their cats, and we shall get along very well."

At this, Princess Elena sprang from under the couch and threw her arms around the bewildered but joyful Raimond. And King Hugo commanded all the bells to be rung for the betrothal of the two lovers.

Instead of being angry at Margot for having tricked

him, King Hugo kept his word, and better. He invited every cat in the kingdom to the wedding; and set out for them tables laden with bowls of cream, platters of fish and fowl, and bouquets of catnip. And Margot, as Maid of Honor, carried the bride's train.

King Hugo also repealed his other foolish laws. Though he grew no fonder of pickled herrings or holidays, he never again forbade them to his subjects. And because he saw to it that all cats were treated with utmost respect, he became known throughout the land as Hugo the Cat-King, a title which hardly pleased him but which he accepted nevertheless.

In gratitude, the Princess would have kept Margot in silks and jewels; but the cat politely declined, saying she was quite comfortable in her own fur. While she stayed with Elena and Raimond happily all their lives, having seen the ways of kings and courtiers, Margot privately judged it far more sensible to be a cat.

The Cat Who Said No

SHIRA-ZAR the Mighty had never in all his life heard the word "No." It was forbidden even to whisper it in his presence, or to disagree with him by so much as a raised eyebrow. To his Master of Royal Revels, Shira-Zar need only say:

"Would it not be amusing to see a thousand elephants dance?"

"Yes, O Magnificent One," the Master of Royal Revels would answer. "Yes, how marvelously amusing!"

And a thousand elephants would straightaway be assembled and made to dance in the Royal Pavilion before Shira-Zar's gold and ivory throne; although Shira-Zar was hardly amused at the damage they caused.

To the Royal Cook, Shira-Zar need only mention:

"Would it not be a refreshing change to have poached hummingbird eggs for breakfast?"

"Yes, Ineffable Potentate," the Royal Cook would answer. "Oh, yes, how joyously refreshing!"

And hummingbird eggs would be immediately sought out and poached precisely as Shira-Zar had ordered;

41

although he felt by no means refreshed when these dainties gave him a severe colic.

Indeed, no matter how extravagant his commands even in matters of state, his Grand Vizier and Royal Council always hailed them as utterances of unmatched wisdom.

Nevertheless, Shira-Zar found his days wearisome and dull. To while away the hours, his courtiers diverted him with games which, of course, he always won. Parcheesi, backgammon, cards, and dice made him yawn. Only one game truly distracted him: the game of chess. Of this he never tired, and each day the greatest chess masters were summoned to match their wits against his. Shrewd and clever players, they were also shrewd and clever enough to lose. One after the other, they were sent away defeated, though laden with costly gifts and favors.

But the day came when Shira-Zar had triumphed over every chess master from high rank to low. Still, he demanded another worthy opponent.

"Yes, Invincible Commander of Rooks and Pawns," replied the Grand Vizier. "Yes, one does remain. It is said that Baraka the cat, in the Shaipur Bazaar, plays chess more cunningly than any in your kingdom."

"Set up the board," said Shira-Zar, "and fetch me this Baraka. It should be moderately amusing to play one game with a bazaar cat and to checkmate him."

Baraka was immediately sent for, and conveyed to the Royal Pavilion in a chair of cedar wood adorned with jewels and draped with gold-embroidered silken curtains. In his bearing, Baraka was no less impressive than his vehicle, for he was a large-framed cat with long,

slate-blue hair and eyes of burnished copper; tufts of fur jutted from both sides of his face, and his long whiskers curled handsomely at the tips.

However, Baraka was not especially pleased at this intrusion on his daily rounds. In Shaipur Bazaar, he made it his business to see that all went as it should; he kept an eye on the doings of the water sellers, the silversmiths, the leathercrafters, and settled disputes among the merchants. He conversed with beggars and charcoal burners, pondered deep questions with visiting scholars; and, when time allowed, meditated in the shade of a coffeeshop awning.

For all his important activities, Baraka could never turn down a game of chess, whoever the opponent; and, knowing of the skill of Shira-Zar, he expected this to be a short one.

The Royal Pavilion was crowded with nobles, ladies of the court, and palace officials all eager to observe the match. A low table had been set before Shira-Zar, and on it a board inlaid with squares of ebony and mother-of-pearl. The chessmen were of crimson cinnabar studded with rubies, and whitest alabaster studded with diamonds. After saluting Shira-Zar with no more nor less than required courtesy, Baraka took his place on the cushions prepared for him.

However, as Shira-Zar was about to open the game, Baraka raised a paw:

"O Guardian of Justice, shall we now draw lots to decide which of us will move first?"

The courtiers murmured at such audacity. Shira-Zar frowned and, before the Grand Vizier could intervene, declared to Baraka:

"Cat, I have already determined that I shall have the first move."

Baraka shrugged. "Since it is your board, your pieces, and your palace, it may as well be your choice. It is all the same to me. The game is the game, and so let us play it."

Again, Shira-Zar was about to begin. Once more, Baraka held up his paw:

"O All-Seeing Eye, surely you have observed that one of my castles is missing?"

The courtiers looked askance at each other and the Grand Vizier glared at Baraka. Shira-Zar scowled and his cheeks flushed. Nevertheless, he grudgingly replaced the missing piece, which he had previously concealed in the palm of his hand.

Satisfied, Baraka allowed the match to proceed. For his part, the cat surveyed the board calmly and moved his pieces thoughtfully and precisely. Shira-Zar, however, soon began to bite his lips and chew his fingernails. He sweated and grumbled and muttered under his breath. He clenched his teeth and stared in disbelief as piece after piece fell to Baraka; and he saw clearly that in one move more the cat would checkmate him.

"Stop," commanded Shira-Zar. "The board shall now be turned between us. I shall play your pieces and you shall play mine."

"O Lion of the Law," said Baraka, "this cannot be done. After all, the game is the game. Change sides in the middle of a match? Indeed, no."

Hearing this, the courtiers gasped in horror. Some clapped their hands over their ears, as if the word had been a red-hot poker jabbed into their heads; the

45

mouths of some fell open, the jaws of others froze shut. The Royal Field Marshal fainted at the shock and had to be sprinkled with rosewater by the Royal Physician. The Grand Vizier, stunned, clutched the arm of the throne to keep himself from collapsing.

Shira-Zar, however, only put his head to one side and gave Baraka a puzzled glance:

"Cat, what was that curious word you spoke? A strange sound: nah . . . nooh . . ."

"Simply 'no,' " replied Baraka. "As I said before, I say again: No."

"Interesting," said Shira-Zar. "In what language is this most peculiar term, and what does it mean?"

Before Baraka could answer, the Royal Interpreter hurried forward:

"Radiant Master of Supreme Syntax," he said, "obviously this cat is speaking in the language of a remote northern province; an obscure tongue, most ungrammatical; archaic as well as obsolete; and phonetically corrupted beyond recognition. I shall compile a dictionary of it for the edification of your Philological Perspicacity. Meanwhile, allow me briefly to explain. Those who employ this vulgar dialect pronounce the letter 'Y' as if it were the letter 'N'—and 'ess' as if it were 'oh.' Therefore, in proper translation and transliteration, this ill-spoken cat is actually saying 'Yes.' "

"I was born in Shaipur Bazaar," said Baraka to the Royal Interpreter, "and have lived all my life there. My language is unmistakably clear: No."

At this, the Royal Physician hastened to the throne, bowed deeply to Shira-Zar; and, before Baraka could protest, thrust a finger into the cat's mouth, peered down his throat, squinted through a magnifying glass into Baraka's ears and eyes, and took his paw between two fingers to count his pulse.

"O Fountain of All Pharmaceutical Wisdom," he said confidently, "with apologies to my learned colleague, it is clear to me this cat suffers from a strangulation of the brain pan, with consequent disorder of the cerebellum. In short, his senses are altogether deranged. While his lower glottis and upper uvula may express a sound resembling 'Nuh-ooh,' this unfortunate victim of delusion and hallucination sincerely believes himself to be saying 'Yes.' For the illumination of Your Diagnostic Delectability, I shall draft a report on this rare medical phenomenon."

Baraka smoothed his ruffled fur. "Physician, I assure you I said what I meant, and meant what I said."

"Somehow," put in Shira-Zar, "I am beginning to think I do not like this word. But the significance still eludes me. Explain immediately."

"Allow me, O Subtle Propounder of Paradox," said the Royal Philosopher. "The resolution of this apparent antinomy lies not in phonetics nor physics, but in philosophy. If we consider negative and positive essences as a cosmological entity instead of irreconcilable antitheses; and especially if we consider that all external objectivity is determined by internal subjectivity, the answer is clear, as I shall set down for Your Metaphysical Magnificence in a special tractatus. Whatever this cat may say, 'Yes' and 'No' are one and the same."

"To you, perhaps," Baraka said, "but not to me."

"This word pleases me less and less," declared Shira-

Zar. "Despite your physics and philosophies, the chessboard has not yet been turned around."

"O Indomitable Intelligence," Baraka said, "now you are beginning to understand."

"Cat," said Shira-Zar in rising anger, "do you tell me by one sound, one breath, one word smaller than a flea, that My Royal Will is not to be obeyed?"

"O Uncontradictable Monarch," answered Baraka, "you have grasped it entirely."

As Shira-Zar had likened the cat's "No" to a flea, he now began to squirm as if this flea had bored into his ear, crept into his brain, there to grow bigger by the moment; and, indeed, was shouting "No" at the top of its voice until the echoes rang and resounded louder and louder. Horrified and furious, he clapped his hands to his head and burst out:

"I do not permit such an answer! Grand Vizier, this cat will be punished!"

"Yes, yes, Implacable Chastiser of Impudence," stammered the Grand Vizier, as horrified as Shira-Zar himself. "Yes, of course. But in what way? In all the history of the kingdom, this has never happened before. Since it has always been considered impossible, even unthinkable, a suitable punishment has never been set down."

"Invent one!" cried Shira-Zar. "Boil him! Pickle him! Roast him! All three at once!"

"O Gentle Dove of Kindliness," Baraka said, "the game is the game, and it still is my move."

Shira-Zar ground his teeth and glowered at the chessboard where the pieces stood exactly as they had been. Distasteful and infuriating though it was, Shira-Zar admitted to himself that Baraka was right. Unless the cat changed both his mind and his answer, his "No" would keep echoing forever in the head of Shira-Zar. So, instead of ordering the cat boiled, pickled, and roasted then and there, Shira-Zar took a deep breath to calm himself, and in a cordial tone addressed Baraka:

"Cat of Shaipur Bazaar, surely you cannot be so foolish and stubborn. How deplorable and unpleasant it would be for you if I were obliged to have you boiled in oil. For the sake of a mere chess match? After all, it is only a game."

"True," said Baraka, "but the finest game in the world."

"Be that as it may," replied Shira-Zar. "Compared with my royal duties, with affairs of high state, this is a small matter; trivial, inconsequential, unworthy of a moment's notice."

"If that be so," answered Baraka, "then why concern yourself with trifles? If it makes no difference one way or the other, the board may just as well stay as it is."

Shira-Zar frowned, pulled at his beard, then cleared his throat and began again:

"Ah—Esteemed Feline, in principle we entirely agree. A passing amusement, soon forgotten. On the other hand, in these particular circumstances, it is of utmost importance."

"If that be so," answered Baraka, "then all the more reason to play correctly."

At this, Shira-Zar was about to explode with fury; but he chewed his lips, rubbed his brow, and did all to keep his temper. A thought had come to him and he whispered urgently to his Grand Vizier.

Baraka, meanwhile, folded his paws and settled him-

50

self on the pillows. As he was considering whether or not to take a nap, again Shira-Zar spoke to him:

"Honored Guest, what a tiring day this has been for you. Are your cushions soft enough? Make yourself comfortable, Exalted Descendant of Tigers."

Even before Shira-Zar finished, Baraka's nose had begun quivering at the delicious aroma wafting through the Royal Pavilion. Reminded that he had missed his morning snack, he licked his lips and his mouth watered; for now he saw a procession of servants enter, bearing platters, trays, bowls, and golden salvers all filled to overflowing with the most exquisite dainties of every kind. Bands of musicians followed, playing sweetly on ouds, rebecs, and gitterns, while troops of dancing girls clashed tiny silver cymbals which they wore like rings on their fingers. The courtiers murmured in wonder at the sight; for never had Shira-Zar offered a banquet rivaling this in luxury and splendor.

"Let us rest and refresh ourselves a little," Shira-Zar continued. "And when you have dined, these damsels will comb you with combs of tortoiseshell, tickle your ears with ostrich plumes, and perfume you with attar of roses. Before that, however, let us take only a fleeting moment to conclude our little pastime."

"Gladly," said Baraka. "But the board stays as it is."

"Why, of course it will, Noblest of All Cats," replied Shira-Zar. "How foolish of me to think of turning the board around. Indeed, it will remain as you see it. We shall merely exchange places; I sit on your side, and you on mine, even upon my throne."

"The game is the game," said Baraka. "No."

Shira-Zar leaped to his feet. "May a herd of wild

51

camels regurgitate on your whiskers! May you grow a thousand pairs of ears and have swarms of earwigs in every one! May your tail stretch from here to the moon with a knot every inch!"

Then he turned to his Grand Vizier and shouted:

"Remove this miserable offspring of rabbits and baboons! Boil him, roast him, pickle him! Turn him into shish-kebab on a skewer!"

"O River of Compassion," said Baraka, "do as you see fit. Only allow me to ask you this: Will making shish-kebab of me change the game by so much as a pawn?"

Shira-Zar hesitated, then protested: "But—but, if I am to win—"

"Win?" replied Baraka. "Tell me, Proud Master of Glorious Gambits, are you truly content with opponents who never oppose you?"

Shira-Zar stared sheepishly at the carpet and in a low voice said to Baraka:

"Between the two of us, Cat, I find it rather dull."

"Are you content, then, with councillors who tell you only what you want to hear?" asked Baraka. "It would seem to me, O Uncontradictable One, that an honest 'No' is worth more than a false 'Yes.'"

Shira-Zar did not answer. However, to his surprise, he found himself growing a little more accustomed to this strange word "No." If at first it had bitten him like a flea, he now found the sensation to be not altogether displeasing; and, in fact, more amusing and refreshing than the dancing elephants or hummingbird eggs. So, at last, he replied:

"Cat, it may be as you say. Henceforth, I command that all speak their minds to me, whether they agree or disagree. As for you, return in peace to Shaipur Bazaar. Though I hope you will permit me to request your advice as needed. My councillors no doubt have the best of intentions but, by and large, I expect your opinions will be more reliable."

"Agreed," said Baraka. "I suppose I can find time to keep an eye on your kingdom as well as Shaipur Bazaar. Nevertheless," he continued, glancing at the chessboard, "there is a matter unfinished between us."

"True," answered Shira-Zar. "The game is the game. Cat, it is your move."

Baraka studied the board carefully for several moments, then advanced a pawn.

"O Most Admirable," said Baraka, "you are checkmated."

"So I am," replied Shira-Zar, with a sigh. "Cat, you have exasperated me beyond belief, aggravated me, spoiled my appetite, and now you have beaten me at my favorite game. At last, are you satisfied?"

And Baraka answered: "Yes."

The Cat and the Golden Egg

QUICKSET, a silver-gray cat, lived with Dame Agnes, a poor widow. Not only was he a cheerful companion, but clever at helping the old woman make ends meet. If the chimney smoked, he tied a bundle of twigs to his tail, climbed up the flue, and cleaned it with all the skill of the town sweep. He sharpened the old woman's knives and scissors, and mended her pots and pans neatly as any tinker. Did Dame Agnes knit, he held the skein of yarn; did she spin, he turned the spinning wheel.

Now, one morning Dame Agnes woke up with a bone-cracking rheumatism. Her joints creaked, her back ached, and her knees were so stiff she could no way get out of bed.

"My poor Quickset," she moaned, "today you and I must both go hungry."

At first, Quickset thought Dame Agnes meant it was the rheumatism that kept her from cooking breakfast, so he answered:

"Go hungry? No, indeed. You stay comfortable; I'll make us a little broiled sausage and soft-boiled egg, and brew a pot of tea for you. Then I'll sit on your lap to warm you, and soon you'll be good as new."

Before Dame Agnes could say another word, he hurried to the pantry. But, opening the cupboard, he saw only bare shelves: not so much as a crust of bread or crumb of cheese; not even a dry bone or bacon rind.

"Mice!" he cried. "Eaten every scrap! They're out of hand, I've been too easy on them. I'll settle accounts with those fellows later. But now, mistress, I had best go to Master Grubble's market and buy what we need."

Dame Agnes thereupon burst into tears. "Oh, Quickset, it isn't mice, it's money. I have no more. Not a penny left for food or fuel."

"Why, mistress, you should have said something about that before now," replied Quickset. "I never would have let you come to such a state. No matter, I'll think of a way to fill your purse again. Meantime, I'll have Master Grubble give us our groceries on credit."

"Grubble? Give credit?" Dame Agnes exclaimed. "You know the only things he gives is short weight at high prices. Alas for the days when the town had a dozen tradesmen and more: a baker, a butcher, a green-grocer, and all the others. But they're gone, thanks to Master Grubble. One by one, he's gobbled them up. Schemed and swindled them out of their businesses! And now he's got the whole town under his thumb, for it's deal with Grubble or deal with no one."

"In that case," replied Quickset, "deal with him I will. Or, to put it better, he'll deal with me."

The old woman shook her head. "You'll still need money. And you shall have it, though I must do something I hoped I'd never have to do.

"Go to the linen chest," Dame Agnes went on. "At

56

the bottom, under the good pillowslips, there's an old wool stocking. Fetch it out and bring it to me."

Puzzled, Quickset did as she asked. He found the stocking with a piece of string tied around the toe and carried it to Dame Agnes, who undid the knot, reached in and drew out one small gold coin.

"Mistress, that's more than enough," said Quickset. "Why did you fret so? With this, we can buy all we want."

Instead of being cheered by the gold piece in her hand, Dame Agnes only sighed:

"This is the last of the small savings my dear husband left to me. I've kept it all these years, and promised myself never to spend it."

"Be glad you did keep it," said Quickset, "for now's the time you need it most."

"I didn't put this by for myself," Dame Agnes replied. "It was for you. I meant to leave it to you in my will. It was to be your legacy, a little something until you found another home. But I see I shall have to spend it. Once gone, it's gone, and that's the end of everything."

At this, Dame Agnes began sobbing again. But Quickset reassured her:

"No need for tears. I'll see to this matter. Only let me have that gold piece a little while. I'll strike such a bargain with Master Grubble that we'll fill our pantry with meat and drink a-plenty. Indeed, he'll beg me to keep the money and won't ask a penny, that I promise."

"Master Grubble, I fear, will be more than a match even for you," Dame Agnes replied. Nevertheless, she did as Quickset urged, put the coin in a leather purse, and hung it around his neck.

Quickset hurried through town to the market, where he found Master Grubble sitting on a high stool behind the counter. For all that his shelves were loaded with victuals of every kind, with meats, and vegetables, and fruits, Grubble looked as though he had never sampled his own wares. There was more fat on his bacon than on himself. He was lean-shanked and sharp-eyed, his nose narrow as a knife blade. His mouth was pursed and puckered as if he had been sipping vinegar, and his cheeks as mottled as moldy cheese. At sight of Quickset, the storekeeper never so much as climbed down from his stool to wait on his customer, but only made a sour face; and, in a voice equally sour, demanded:

"And what do you want? Half a pound of mouse tails? A sack of catnip? Out! No loitering! I don't cater to the cat trade."

Despite this curdled welcome, Quickset bowed and politely explained that Dame Agnes was ailing and he had come shopping in her stead.

"Sick she must be," snorted Master Grubble, "to send a cat marketing, without even a shopping basket. How do you mean to carry off what you buy? Push it along the street with your nose?"

"Why sir," Quickset answered, "I thought you might send your shop boy around with the parcels. I'm sure you'll do it gladly when you see the handsome order to be filled. Dame Agnes needs a joint of beef, a shoulder of mutton, five pounds of your best sausage, a dozen of the largest eggs—"

"Not so fast," broke in the storekeeper. "Joints and shoulders, is it? Sausage and eggs? Is that what you want? Then I'll tell you what I want: cash on the

59

counter, paid in full. Or you, my fine cat, won't have so much as a wart from one of my pickles."

"You'll be paid," Quickset replied, "and very well paid. But now I see your prices, I'm not sure I brought enough money with me."

"So that's your game!" cried Grubble. "Well, go and get enough. I'll do business with you then, and not before."

"It's a weary walk home and back again," said Quickset. "Allow me a minute or two and I'll have money to spare. And, Master Grubble, if you'd be so kind as to lend me an egg."

"Egg?" retorted Grubble. "What's that to do with paying my bill?"

"You'll see," Quickset answered. "I guarantee you'll get all that's owing to you."

Grubble at first refused and again ordered Quickset from the shop. Only when the cat promised to pay double the price of the groceries, as well as an extra fee for the use of the egg, did the storekeeper grudgingly agree.

Taking the egg from Master Grubble, Quickset placed it on the floor, then carefully settled himself on top of it.

"Fool!" cried Grubble. "What are you doing? Get off my egg! This cat's gone mad, and thinks he's a chicken!"

Quickset said nothing, but laid back his ears and waved his tail, warning Grubble to keep silent. After another moment, Quickset got up and brought the egg to the counter:

"There, Master Grubble, that should be enough."

"What?" shouted the storekeeper. "Idiot cat! You mean to pay me with my own egg?"

"With better than that, as you'll see," answered Quickset. While Grubble fumed, Quickset neatly cracked the shell and poured the contents into a bowl. At this, Grubble ranted all the more:

"Alley rabbit! Smash my egg, will you? I'll rub your nose in it!"

Suddenly Master Grubble's voice choked in his gullet. His eyes popped as he stared into the bowl. There, with the broken egg, lay a gold piece.

Instantly, he snatched it out. "What's this?"

"What does it look like?" returned Quickset.

Grubble squinted at the coin, flung it onto the counter and listened to it ring. He bit it, peered closer, turned it round and round in his fingers, and finally blurted:

"Gold!"

Grubble, in his fit of temper, had never seen Quickset slip the coin from the purse and deftly drop it into the bowl. Awestruck, he gaped at the cat, then lowered his voice to a whisper:

"How did you do that?"

Quickset merely shook his head and shrugged his tail. At last, as the excited storekeeper pressed him for an answer, he winked one eye and calmly replied:

"Now, now, Master Grubble, a cat has trade secrets just as a storekeeper. I don't ask yours, you don't ask mine. If I told you how simple it is, you'd know as much as I do. And if others found out—"

"Tell me!" cried Grubble. "I won't breathe a word to a living soul. My dear cat, listen to me," he hurried on.

61

"You'll have all the victuals you want. For a month! A year! Forever! Here, this very moment, I'll have my boy take a carload to your mistress. Only teach me to sit on eggs as you did."

"Easily done," said Quickset. "But what about that gold piece?"

"Take it!" cried Grubble, handing the coin to Quickset. "Take it, by all means."

Quickset pretended to think over the bargain, then answered:

"Agreed. But you must do exactly as I tell you."

Grubble nodded and his eyes glittered. "One gold piece from one egg. But what if I used two eggs? Or three, or four, or five?"

"As many as you like," said Quickset. "A basketful, if it suits you."

Without another moment's delay, Grubble called his boy from the storeroom and told him to deliver all that Quickset ordered to the house of Dame Agnes. Then, whimpering with pleasure, he filled his biggest basket with every egg in the store. His nose twitched, his hands trembled, and his usually sallow face turned an eager pink.

"Now," said Quickset, "so you won't be disturbed, take your basket to the top shelf and sit on it there. One thing more, the most important. Until those eggs hatch, don't say a single word. If you have anything to tell me, whatever the reason, you must only cluck like a chicken. Nothing else, mind you. Cackle all you like; speak but once, and the spell is broken."

"What about my customers? Who's to wait on them?"

asked Grubble, unwilling to lose business even in exchange for a fortune.

"Never fear," said Quickset. "I'll mind the store."

"What a fine cat you are," purred Grubble. "Noble animal. Intelligent creature."

With that, gleefully chuckling and licking his lips, he clambered to the top shelf, hauling his heavy burden along with him. There he squatted gingerly over the basket, so cramped that he was obliged to draw his knees under his chin and fold his arms as tightly as he could; until indeed he looked much like a skinny, long-beaked chicken hunched on a nest.

Below, Quickset no sooner had taken his place on the stool than Mistress Libbet, the carpenter's wife, stepped through the door.

"Why, Quickset, what are you doing here?" said she. "Have you gone into trade? And can that be Master Grubble on the shelf? I swear he looks as if he's sitting on a basket of eggs."

"Pay him no mind," whispered Quickset. "He fancies himself a hen. An odd notion, but harmless. However, since Master Grubble is busy nesting, I'm tending shop for him. So, Mistress Libbet, how may I serve you?"

"There's so much our little ones need." Mistress Libbet sighed unhappily. "And nothing we can afford to feed them. I was hoping Master Grubble had some scraps or trimmings."

"He has much better," said Quickset, pulling down one of the juiciest hams and slicing away at it with Grubble's carving knife. "Here's a fine bargain today: only a penny a pound."

Hearing this, Master Grubble was about to protest, but caught himself in the nick of time. Instead, he began furiously clucking and squawking:

"Cut-cut-cut! Aw-cut!"

"What's that you say?" Quickset glanced up at the agitated storekeeper and cupped an ear with his paw. "Cut more? Yes, yes, I understand. The price is still too high? Very well, if you insist: two pounds for a penny."

Too grateful to question such generosity on the part of Grubble, Mistress Libbet flung a penny onto the counter and seized her ham without waiting for Quickset to wrap it. As she hurried from the store, the tailor's wife and the stonecutter's daughter came in; and, a moment later, Dame Gerton, the laundrywoman.

"Welcome, ladies," called Quickset. "Welcome, one and all. Here's fine prime meats, fine fresh vegetables on sale today. At these prices, they won't last long. So, hurry! Step up!"

As the delighted customers pressed eagerly toward the counter, Master Grubble's face changed from sallow to crimson, from crimson to purple. Cackling frantically, he waggled his head and flapped his elbows against his ribs.

"Cut-aw-cut!" he bawled. "Cut-cut-aw! Cuck-cuck! Cock-a-doodle-do!"

Once more, Quickset made a great show of listening carefully:

"Did I hear you a-right, Master Grubble? Give all? Free? What a generous soul you are"

With that, Quickset began hurling meats, cheese, vegetables, and loaves of sugar into the customers' outstretched baskets. Grubble's face now turned from purple to bilious green. He crowed, clucked, brayed, and bleated until he sounded like a barnyard gone mad.

"Give more?" cried Quickset. "I'm doing my best!"

"Cut-aw!" shouted Grubble and away went a chain of sausages. "Ak-ak-cut-aak!" And away went another joint of beef. At last, he could stand no more:

"Stop! Stop!" he roared. "Wretched cat! You'll drive me out of business!"

Beside himself with fury, Master Grubble forgot his cramped quarters and sprang to his feet. His head struck the ceiling and he tumbled back into the basket of eggs. As he struggled to free himself from the flood of shattered yolks, the shelf cracked beneath him and he went plummeting headlong into a barrel of flour.

"Robber!" stormed Grubble, crawling out and shaking a fist at Quickset. "Swindler! You promised I'd hatch gold from eggs!"

"What's that?" put in the tailor's wife. "Gold from eggs? Master Grubble, you're as foolish as you're greedy."

"But a fine cackler," added the laundrywoman, flapping her arms. "Let's hear it again, your cut-cut-awk!"

"I warned you not to speak a word," Quickset told the storekeeper, who was egg-soaked at one end and floured at the other. "But you did. And so you broke the spell. Why, look at you, Master Grubble. You nearly turned yourself into a dipped pork chop. Have a care. Someone might fry you."

With that, Quickset went home to breakfast.

As for Master Grubble, when word spread that he had been so roundly tricked, and so easily, he became such a laughingstock that he left town and was never seen again. At the urging of the townsfolk, Dame Agnes and Quickset took charge of the market, and ran it well and fairly. All agreed that Quickset was the cleverest cat in the world. And, since Quickset had the same opinion, it was surely true.

The Cobbler and His Cat

THERE WAS a cobbler named Shubin, whose uncle died and left him a good sum of money; no great fortune, but more than Shubin ever had in his life.

"Vaska," he told his black-and-white cat, "we're rich, you and I. Now we must do like the gentry, and live up to our new station."

"My old one suits me well enough," replied Vaska. "What the gentry do is their business, and what I do is mine. I'll stick to being a cobbler's cat, and I advise you: Stick to being a cobbler."

"What nonsense you're talking," retorted Shubin. "Who ever heard of a rich man who didn't act like one? And so must I. Otherwise, I'd be taken for a fool."

Until then, Shubin had been content with bread and cheese, groats and cabbage. Now, for dinner, he sent round after bottles of wine, joints of beef, smoked herring, roast chickens, and a hamper of pastries. Even Vaska, with his keen appetite, soon had more than his fill.

"Shubin, what are you doing?" cried the cat, seeing his master, stuffed to bursting, tossing the rest of the food out the shop window. "There's enough to last us a week and more."

"As gentry don't eat leftovers, neither will I," answered the cobbler, who then began spinning around, bowing, capering, waving his arms in the air, and stamping his feet on the floor.

"Now what are you up to?" demanded Vaska, afraid so much food and drink had sent his master into a fit.

"Dancing," gasped the cobbler. "The gentry always have a little dancing after a feast. It's hot and heavy work, I must say. No matter. It's to be done, so I'll do it."

Next day, once he got over a terrible bellyache, Shubin took Vaska to the tailor and had himself and his cat measured for suits of clothes, silk breeches, and embroidered waistcoats; then to the hairdresser, where he ordered a huge powdered wig for himself and a smaller one for Vaska.

"It's not my idea of comfort," Shubin admitted, "but, as this is what the gentry wear, I'll do no less."

Vaska, however, refused point-blank to don such apparel, no matter how his master pleaded, insisted, or commanded.

"Foolish cat!" Shubin cried. "You can't go about in that shabby fur!"

"Better fur that fits," replied Vaska, "than fancy silk that never will."

Grumbling that Vaska would never make a gentleman, the cobbler went back to the shop. There, he opened a box of snuff he had bought at the tobacco dealer's and set about cramming the contents up his nose.

70

"Stop it! Stop it!" cried Vaska, choking on the clouds of brown powder swirling around Shubin's head.

"I can't!" choked the cobbler, sneezing madly and wiping his streaming eyes. "If snuff's good enough for the gentry's noses, it must be good enough for mine."

And he kept on packing snuff into his nose until the box was empty and he sneezed his way to bed.

Next morning, when Shubin came to breakfast, instead of greeting Vaska as usual he launched into such a spate of gibberish that the bewildered cat clapped his paws over his ears.

"That snuff's gone into your brains!" cried Vaska. "You're jabbering like a maniac. I can't make out a word you say."

"Stupid cat," returned Shubin, "I'm speaking French. And you must learn to speak it as well as I do. Then, we can talk to each other in fine high style."

"High style, low style, or whatever," answered Vaska, "we can talk to each other as we did before, and understand each other a lot better."

Next, nothing would do but Shubin had to have a horse and carriage. But, since he had no stable, he was obliged to knock down part of his shop so he could lodge the animal and vehicle. However, since he had nowhere to go in the carriage, he spent much of the day galloping round and round. As Vaska refused to serve as coachman, Shubin had to hold the reins himself. When he came back, having upset the greengrocer's vegetable stand, sent the poultryman's geese flying, and run over the toes of a dozen of his neighbors, Vaska was waiting with a sheaf of papers.

"Look at these bills," declared the cat. "The tailor, the victualer, the wine merchant—"

"Out the window with them!" cried Shubin. "Who ever heard of a rich man paying his tailor? Or paying anyone else, for the matter of that!"

Saying this, Shubin tucked in his chin, tilted back his head as far as it would go, and stared down his nose so intently that his eyes crossed.

"Shubin, what's wrong with you?" exclaimed Vaska. "Have you a crick in the neck?"

"Have you ever seen how the gentry stare at common folk?" replied the cobbler, trying to speak without moving his jaw. "It isn't easy, let me tell you. But never mind, I'll soon have the knack of it."

Until then, Shubin had been industrious and accommodating with his customers. Now he left the running of the shop to Vaska, insisting it would look foolish for a man of his wealth to bother cobbling boots and mending soles. Instead, he sat up till all hours, stayed abed past noon; then went about with his nose packed with snuff, sneezing in French, sighing and moaning over the heavy burdens and responsibilities of being rich.

Shubin also decided that he required visiting cards reading:

HIS EXCELLENCY THE HONORABLE SHUBIN,
PURVEYOR OF ADORNMENTS
FOR NETHER EXTREMITIES

However, on his way to the printer to order these cards, he overheard the baker and the carpenter talking together:

"That Shubin," said the baker, shaking his head, "how he does take on. The fellow's lost his wits, if he ever had any to begin with. He's a fool, that's one thing certain."

"Ah, that Shubin," said the carpenter, "he's one of the great idiots of this world. So says everyone. Why, all agree that even his cat is wiser than he is."

At this, Shubin was so taken aback and so put out that he turned around and ran home, red-faced with indignation and humiliation, and told Vaska what he had heard.

"How can this be true?" stammered Shubin. "You, wiser than I? But, if everyone says it, then true it must be. Vaska, you're hiding something from me. You know something I don't know."

"Maybe I do, maybe I don't," replied the cat. "Wise isn't for me to say. Anyone who calls himself wise is a fool to begin with."

This answer only convinced Shubin that indeed his cat knew more than he was telling, and he replied:

"Vaska, I want you to make me as wise as you are. Who ever heard of a cat more clever than his master, especially a master as rich and elegant as I? Let's have it, now. Out with it!"

And so he kept at it and at it, first shouting, then wheedling, then staring impressively down his nose; and, all in all, doing everything he could to winkle out Vaska's secret.

"Very well," the cat said at last. "On the stroke of midnight, you come along with me and find out for yourself. But you must watch me closely and, no matter who, do all that I do."

Shubin eagerly agreed, and waited impatiently for midnight. Then, on the stroke of twelve from the town clock, Vaska unlatched the door and slipped out into the street, the cobbler trotting after.

"Here, now, Shubin," called Vaska, stopping a moment and glancing back. "I told you to do as I do. So, down you go on all fours."

Shubin had not expected this; but, having begun, he was more eager than ever; and, without question or protest, he crouched down as Vaska ordered. Being a little stout around the middle, he managed only with difficulty. Nevertheless, puffing and sweating, he scuttled along behind Vaska, always keeping his eyes on the white tip of the cat's tail.

"Not so fast," panted Shubin. "I'm not the right shape for this kind of work."

Vaska, meanwhile, loped silently into one of the back alleys. Shubin scrambled after him, stumbling over empty bottles, lurching against barrels of rubbish, and making such a clatter that Vaska hissed at him to be more quiet.

"That's all very well for you to say," complained Shubin. "You've got pads on your paws. I have to scrape along on my hands and knees."

But Vaska never slackened his pace and went swiftly down one crooked alley after another. And now it was so dark that Shubin could no longer glimpse the tip of the cat's tail. Even so, the cobbler plunged on, as blind as if he had a sack over his head. A moment later, he was jolted back on his heels. Shubin howled in pain and clapped his hands to his pate, which throbbed as if it had cracked in two. If he could see nothing before, now stars and comets danced in front of his eyes; for he had fetched up, with all speed, hard against a brick wall.

"Stupid cat!" moaned Shubin, rubbing his head and blinking until he could just barely make out Vaska perched on the wall. "What are you trying to do to me? I might have knocked my brains out! I can't see my hand in front of my face."

"That's odd," replied Vaska. "Everything's clear as day to me. Come on, Shubin, up you go. And stay close or I can't answer for what happens to you."

Head still reeling and ringing, the cobbler scrambled up the wall. There, he could see a bit more clearly; though what he saw made him groan in dismay. Vaska, calmly and easily, was threading his way over the narrow top of the wall.

"Wait, wait!" pleaded Shubin. "It's enough you had me break my head. Now do you want me to break my neck, into the bargain?"

As Vaska paid no heed to his complaints, Shubin was obliged to scuttle after him; though at every few steps, the cobbler lost his balance and went pitching headfirst off one side or the other. Each time, Vaska ordered him to clamber up again.

"Shubin," said the cat, "I'm beginning to think they're quite right in what they say about you. The youngest kitten would put you to shame."

"What do you take me for?" wailed the cobbler. "I'm not some kind of tightrope walker like you."

Vaska set off again and Shubin teetered along as best he could, telling himself his future wisdom would more than make up for his present pains. But no sooner had he gone a few yards than the wall suddenly dropped away, and he and Vaska tumbled to the cobblestones below.

While plummeting down, Vaska with no effort at all

righted himself to land lightly on his four paws; whereas the unlucky cobbler thudded to the ground like a sack of potatoes, rattling every bone in his body and every tooth in his head.

"Shubin," said the cat, "I really don't know what I'm going to do about you. If you manage no better than that, I'll have to send you home."

Shubin, whose heavy landing had knocked the wind out of him, had no breath to spare for an answer. He crept on, grateful that Vaska now chose to stay on solid footing. Soon, however, they came to a board fence, too high even for the cat to scale. Undismayed, Vaska nosed around until he found a gap in the planking and easily jumped through. Shubin followed; but, unlike Vaska, who had calculated the size of the opening to the very breadth of his whiskers, Shubin got no more than his head and shoulders into the breach. By the time he realized his mistake, he was tightly wedged in the middle and could go neither forward nor back.

"Don't dawdle," said the cat. "Had I known you were such a poor judge of your own girth, I never would have brought you with me."

"I don't carry a yardstick," grunted Shubin, twisting and turning, and doing all he could to squeeze himself through.

"Nor do I," said Vaska. "Mine's in my head. What may be in yours is anyone's guess."

Shubin gritted his teeth, strained and sweated, twisted and wriggled all the more. At last, like a cork out of a bottle, he popped through the fence, leaving behind shreds of clothing but gaining a rich crop of splinters.

"Silence!" hissed the cat, as Shubin began moaning

over his torn breeches and smarting skin. "Get down, flat as you can."

The cobbler squinted in the direction Vaska indicated. By the watery moonlight, he glimpsed half-a-dozen burly tomcats crouching in a circle, looking daggers at each other through their huge glittering eyes. Their ears were notched, their fur torn away in patches, their whiskers thicker than handspikes, and their heads big as cabbages. Never before had Shubin seen such terrifying creatures; though, indeed, never before had he gone crawling through back alleys in the middle of the night.

"Rough customers," whispered Vaska. "Best we stay clear of those fellows."

Gulping and trembling, Shubin breathed easily only after Vaska had led him well away from the hooligans. Passing through a vegetable patch, Vaska halted and jumped onto a barrelhead. Shubin recognized the place as the backyard of Matushka Matrovna, the laundry-woman; and when he asked the cat why they were stopping, Vaska replied:

"A charming little brown tabby lives here. It would be an unforgivable discourtesy if I didn't pay my respects."

With that, Vaska raised his head, arched his whiskers, and began a serenade of melodious miauling. "You join in, too, Shubin," he ordered, leaving off his song for a moment. "Otherwise, the dear creature will be terribly offended."

The cobbler at first protested, but when Vaska reminded him of their agreement there was nothing Shubin could do but settle on his haunches and go to caterwauling at the top of his voice.

No sooner had he started than the shutters of the

upper window burst open. Instead of the little brown tabby, however, the laundrywoman in her nightgown leaned out, shaking a fist and crying:

"Stop that yowling! Scat, scat! Away with you!"

Vaska boldly kept on with his serenade, so Shubin was obliged to do likewise. Temper mounting by the instant, the laundrywoman peered down into the shadows to catch a dim sight of the cobbler.

"Heaven spare us!" she cried. "There's the biggest cat in all this world!"

Fearing the laundrywoman might recognize him and thus have all the more reason to call him a fool, Shubin judged his best hope was to keep to his guise:

"Meow!" bawled the cobbler, as cat-like as he was able. "Meow! Yeow! Arreow-ow-ow!"

"Impudent beast" cried Matushka Matrovna. "You're as brazen as you're big! Meow, is it? I'll give you a meow you'll not forget!"

Before Shubin knew what was happening, Matushka Matrovna fetched a tub of laundry water and tipped it over the windowsill. Vaska jumped instantly aside; but the slow-moving cobbler failed to escape the soapy cascade pouring down on him. Soaked to the skin, half-drowned, sputtering out great soap bubbles, he tried to scramble to his feet, but only tumbled back into the slippery puddle.

To make matters worse, drawn by Vaska's serenade and furious at the intrusion on their domain, the hooligan cats came streaking into the yard, yowling murderously. To the terrified Shubin, their flashing teeth and claws looked as sharp as sabers, their tails lashed like whips, and their yellow eyes blazed like torches.

"On guard, Shubin!" cried Vaska. "Defend yourself! Bush out your hair! Arch your back! Fight or fly!"

Following his own advice, Vaska swelled himself up, curved his back like a drawn bow, and so spiked out his fur that he looked three times his usual size. Shubin, with barely enough hair to fringe his crown, reckoned his best and only defense lay in his legs. Giving up any notion of going on all fours, as Vaska first had ordered, and judging that the greatest wisdom at this particular moment suggested saving his skin, he jumped up and bolted for home as though a horde of cabbage-headed cutthroats were at his heels.

Taking wrong turn after wrong turn, losing himself in the dark and twisting alleyways, at last he found the right path and never slackened his pace until he was back safe in his shop, with the door bolted behind him.

Swift though Shubin had been, Vaska had been swifter; for there was the cat, not a whisker out of place, calmly sitting at the fireside.

"Oh, there you are, Shubin," remarked Vaska. "What kept you? Any cat can find the way home. But you seem a bit wilted. Put yourself at ease, you poor fellow, and I'll make you a glass of tea."

"What of those devil-cats?" blurted Shubin. "Those assassins!"

"No harm done," said Vaska. "We came to an understanding."

Once sure that Vaska was unharmed, Shubin relieved his own distress by taking a stern tone with the cat:

"For shame, Vaska! You had me believe you'd tell me your secret. But no, you lead me on a wild goose chase —or cat chase, or whatever you want to call it. And expect me to do what I'm in no way suited for? Act like a cat? Why not ask me to flap my arms and sail through the air like a bird! Ah, Vaska, that was unkind. You did it on purpose, only to make a fool of me."

Shubin hesitated, then muttered sheepishly:

"That's to say: a greater fool than I was already."

"Cheer up, Shubin," replied the cat. "Make a fool of you? On the contrary. Now, at least you've a reasonable chance of making a wise man of yourself. But, Shubin, one thing I beg you. Please get rid of that foul-smelling snuff. If you must have something to stuff up your nose, try a little catnip."

Not only did Shubin throw out his snuff, but his powdered wig along with it. He put back his leather apron, and folded away his fancy breeches and waistcoat; and wore them only for merrymaking at the town fair and on Vaska's birthday. He used his horse and carriage to deliver his wares, for his business grew better and better; though now his visiting cards read simply:

SHUBIN. COBBLER.

The Painter's Cat

THREE town councillors met one day to consider the finest gift they could bestow on their good people of Roosendaal-op-Zoom.

"I have studied the question carefully," declared Councillor Trumble, "in the light of my profound knowledge and long experience, and there is no doubt in my mind what our gift should be. The cobblestones in Market Street are old, worn, and loose. Therefore, the only wise decision is for each of us to pay a share and have new cobbles laid. Not that I mean to take personal credit for this excellent thought, but in all modesty and humility I suggest the street be renamed: Great Trumble Street."

So saying, he leaned back in his chair, folded his hands over his ample waistcoat, and waited for his colleagues to agree with him. No sooner had Councillor Trumble finished, however, than Councillor De Groot immediately protested:

"My dear sir, it astonishes me to hear such a proposal from one who claims such deep wisdom. New cobblestones? Why, it's only a matter of time until they're as old, worn, and loose as the ones we have already. No, no," he went on, twirling his black mustache, of which he was inordinately fond, "the finest gift, a truly elegant one, is: a pleasure garden, where our good people can stroll at their leisure, to greet one another, to see and be seen. And, if you were to insist, I should raise no objection to naming it: De Groot Gardens."

"Gardens, indeed!" blustered Councillor Vorwick, thrusting out his chin ferociously. "Who strolls when it rains? Or snows? Or after dark? Or during the day, when all are at work? Would you have us waste our guilders on something of so little use? You, De Groot, no doubt would enjoy strutting there, showing off your fancy breeches, or plumed hat, or whatever frippery. And curling that mustache of yours. It's not gardens we need. It's guards! We must share the cost of setting up a company of night watchmen, all in fine uniforms. As you'll need a fearless captain to lead them, I volunteer. Naturally, the company will be known as: Vorwick's Guards."

"Nonsense!" retorted Councillor Trumble, ruffled at having both his wisdom and his cobblestones denied. "I quite agree, a public garden would be an extravagance. Night watchmen even more so! They'd be on duty only half the time! And who'd see their fine uniforms in the dark?"

So the councillors wrangled back and forth, arguing for and against a horse trough in the market place, a bell in the belfry, or a clock in the tower of the town hall; until, after many long hours, at last they agreed. As men of substance, gravity, and public spirit, whose unselfish service the folk of Roosendaal-op-Zoom would surely

84

wish to commemorate, they concluded that their finest, most thoughtful, and valuable gift would be nothing less than a portrait of themselves.

Beaming in satisfaction over their gracious decision, they hurried to the town painter, Master Van Eck, named a sum, and charged him to begin this portrait without delay. Master Van Eck's trade being regrettably slack, he was more than eager to paint a large picture in a short time at a small price. And so he would have done, had it not been for his brindled cat, Hillesum.

This Hillesum was a quick-witted and diligent cat who helped his master grind his pigments, clean his brushes, and ready his palette. As an artist, Van Eck naturally had no head for business, or indeed much else, and could hardly think to lace his boots or button his jacket in the morning; and so Hillesum kept his accounts, cooked the meals, and saw that all was in order. Hearing what fee the councillors offered, Hillesum came forward and respectfully declared:

"Good sirs, I fear you've misunderstood. That will be the cost to each of you; and very reasonable it is, far less than the price for three separate pictures."

"But this is only one picture," Councillor Trumble protested.

"Yes, but there will be three heads and three bodies," countered Hillesum, "and thus three times the work."

"But only one piece of canvas," put in De Groot.

"And only one frame," said Vorwick.

"Yes, but very large ones," replied Hillesum, "with three times the amount of paint needed, not to mention wear and tear on the brushes."

The councillors dickered and bargained with Hillesum and finally settled on a fair price, which, thanks to the cat, was considerably higher than it otherwise would have been. However, when Master Van Eck suggested that the three come each day to sit for their portrait, Councillor Trumble puffed indignantly:

"What, waste my valuable time in a painter's workshop? My civic duties require all my thought and attention."

To which Councillor De Groot added:

"Surely, my bearing, manner, and features are unforgettable."

"And if your memory does falter," said Councillor Vorwick, "you can come and watch me exercising at the fencing academy."

Not wishing to lose the commission, Van Eck agreed and promised to do his best. However, once his clients had left, the painter collapsed onto a stool and stared at the empty canvas on his easel.

"Ah, Hillesum," he cried, "how shall I do? I have no models to work from."

"Never fear," said Hillesum. "Cats have sharp eyes, and none sharper than mine. I had a close look at our three good councillors. So, start your canvas and, if need be, I'll help you."

Much relieved at this, Van Eck did as Hillesum advised. He sketched first in charcoal, then laid in his colors; and Hillesum, keeping a careful eye on the work, added touches here and there. For the cat, having long observed his master, was as clever a painter as Van Eck himself, and even more so: because, for the smaller details, Hillesum could use the tip of his long and flexible tail, finer and more sensitive than any sable brush. So, between the two of them, the painter and his cat began what promised to be a very creditable portrait.

However, when the councillors returned to see what had so far been done, instead of praising Van Eck's efforts they instantly complained:

"Outrageous!" Trumble huffed. "You've put half my face in the shadow!"

"You've set me behind the other two," snapped Vorwick, "so I look smaller than both!"

"Careless work!" put in De Groot. "My waistcoat and ruffles show to no advantage whatever."

So, Van Eck and Hillesum had it all to do over. Even at that, when the councillors came again they were no better pleased:

"You must show me holding a law book," Trumble ordered, "or some volume of philosophy, to represent a powerful mind at work."

"Put a saber in my hand," said Vorwick, "befitting one of my courage and daring."

"It needs more elegance of style," said De Groot. "You must give my jacket a fashionable cut."

Once again, Van Eck and Hillesum scraped away the paint and began afresh. But the councillors were still dissatisfied. Trumble's weighty tome must now have its title in Latin—though the councillor confessed, reluctantly, that he knew not a word of the language. The saber of Vorwick needed to flash more brightly—though Vorwick admitted he had never owned such a blade. And De Groot insisted on gold buttons for his jacket, along with a set of diamond studs—for he judged it thriftier to have them painted than to buy them from the jeweler.

"Far be it from me to tell a tradesman his task," said Councillor Trumble. "But you painters are supposed to be fellows of spirit and vision, are you not? Vision, Master Van Eck, vision! How else reflect our true natures?"

"Quite so," agreed Councillor Vorwick. "I was about to suggest making room in the picture for a horse."

"And a gold watch and chain for me," added Councillor De Groot, "and a few more rings on my fingers, while you're at it."

Thus went each visit from Van Eck's demanding clients, to such a point that he grew more and more agitated, painting feverishly with the wrong end of his brush, dropping his palette, and spilling more paint on his cat than he ever put on his canvas. Had it not been for Hillesum, who never let the councillors' complaints and criticisms ruffle so much as a whisker, Van Eck would have thrown his hands up in despair, and the portrait out the window.

At last, the work was done. But when the councillors came to view it, Trumble gravely shook his head:

"Do you call that a portrait, Master Van Eck? You've put all your time and paint into trifles, and lost the most important. Look how you've shown me! I ask you, is that a noble brow? Is that the gaze of a man of wisdom and sagacity? I see nothing of my prudence, foresight, or generosity—not to mention my humility."

"I'm a painter, not a magician!" cried Van Eck. "I paint what I see. If I can't see it, I can't paint it!"

"That's a narrow-minded attitude," answered Trumble. "Paint what you see, indeed! If that were all, we might as well have hired a house painter instead of an artist."

"My saber looks keener than I do," snorted Vorwick. "Where's my flashing eye? My brave glance?"

"Very slipshod work," said De Groot. "I'm not one to flatter myself, but only repeat what I've been told: There's no finer figure of a man, nor a handsomer pair of mustaches in all the town. But you'd never know it from that picture."

Bombarded from all sides with such complaints, Van Eck tried to defend his work as best he could; but grew so distracted and beside himself, he could only babble incoherently; and even Hillesum could do nothing to change the councillors' opinions.

"This is your last chance, Master Van Eck," Trumble declared, shaking a finger at the distraught painter. "We shall come back at noon tomorrow. By then, if the portrait is not done to our satisfaction, not one guilder will you have from us."

The councillors, for once in full accord, turned on their heels and left Master Van Eck stammering, tearing his hair, and trembling so violently that Hillesum feared the painter would never hold a brush again.

"I should have kept to painting cabbages and turnips!" wailed Van Eck. "Bowls of fruit and plates of herring! Apples don't ask to be pears! Kippers don't try to be critics!"

"Perhaps I know our good councillors better than you do," said Hillesum. "Leave the painting to me."

"Too late!" cried Van Eck. "There's nothing more can be done. I'm already out of pocket for paint and canvas.

90

By tomorrow noon, I'll be out of business as well. Once they spread the word, I'll never have another commission. I'll be lucky to scrape out a living painting signboards for taverns!"

At that, the despairing Van Eck threw down his palette and stamped on it, scattered his brushes in every direction, and kicked over his easel. Then, as any sensible artist would do in the circumstances, he flung himself into his bed, pulled the covers over his head, and vowed he would stay there the rest of his days.

Hillesum was not so easily disheartened. While his master moaned and sniveled, wishing all manner of plagues, toothaches, and scrofulas for his clients, and for himself wishing he had gone into the carpentry trade, the cat went promptly to the task of repainting the portrait.

Never stopping a moment, Hillesum set about his work with all speed. He plied the brushes with both forepaws, dipped his tail into the pots of color; and for the most delicate strokes, used his long whiskers.

As Hillesum could see as well in darkness as in daylight, he stayed at the easel throughout the night. Though Van Eck appeared determined to keep his word and keep to his bed, the cat's industry more than made up for his master's absence. Just before noon, Hillesum draped a cloth over the painting and made ready to welcome the councillors.

These dignitaries were as punctual as they had been difficult to please, arriving precisely at twelve o'clock, when Hillesum had barely finished washing the paint from his paws, tail, and whiskers. Seeing nothing of Master Van Eck, they demanded to know where he was;

and when Hillesum explained the painter had taken to his bed, they looked more disgruntled than before.

"An irresponsible, lazy lot, these artists," said Trumble. "With an important civic project still in hand, your master chooses to snore away his time."

"He was warned," added Vorwick. "No painting, no payment; and that's our last word."

"Sirs, one moment, please," replied Hillesum. "Your portrait is done to perfection. I myself finished it during the night."

"You?" retorted Councillor De Groot. "We demand good art for good money, not cat-scratches."

"Gentlemen, you must understand," said Hillesum, "that my master entrusts only his most extraordinary canvases to my special skill. There are certain fine perceptions, and subtle qualities we cats can see more clearly than you humans. I've made every effort to show you in proper style. If I'm to be reproached for anything, it will be for flattering you."

Still grumbling, the councillors reluctantly seated themselves as Hillesum urged them to do. He then stepped to the easel and pulled away the cloth concealing the portrait.

"There, good sirs," Hillesum proudly declared, with a sweeping gesture of his paw, "a masterpiece if I call it so myself."

"Masterpiece?" cried Trumble, springing to his feet the instant he glimpsed the canvas. "Wretch! You should be put in the stocks!"

"How dare you!" shouted Vorwick, bristling fiercely and shaking a fist at Hillesum. "You should be drummed out of town!"

"Flatter us?" De Groot burst out, his face turning crimson. "Brazen mockery! Gross impudence!"

Hillesum, they saw, had kept all that Van Eck had painted, except for the councillors' faces. And these he had redone with utmost care, transforming them into cats.

Councillor Trumble, in somber garb and Latin text in hand, now had the features of a solemn gray cat with magisterial tufts of fur at his jaws. Councillor De Groot, painted in all his finery, appeared as a sleek, handsome orange-and-white; and Councillor Vorwick, a tiger-striped tom, battle-scarred, with a notch in one ear.

"You asked for vision, gentlemen," said Hillesum, "and there you have it. I confess to a certain artistic license; but had I painted you as you are, I fear you might not have been so pleased."

"What are you talking about?" retorted Vorwick. "Paint us as we are? That's exactly what you should have done."

"Indeed?" Hillesum replied. "Knowing what I know? You must realize, we cats gossip among ourselves, as you do. However, our gossip stays closer to the facts than does yours. As for your bravery, I have it on the excellent authority of your own kitchen cat that you were terrified into fits when a mouse ran through your bed chamber one night.

"Councillor De Groot, you're a fine figure of a man," went on Hillesum, "as you yourself are the first to admit. Yet I hear that you touch up your mustache with boot blacking; and last week, when you were caught in the rain, you had to dash home with all haste, for fear it would wash off. And, Councillor Trumble, isn't it true, for all your wisdom, that you bought a bit of glass from a passing peddler who assured you it was a priceless diamond?"

"Did you, indeed?" asked Vorwick of the flustered councillor. "A child of two has better sense!"

"Braggart!" sputtered Trumble. "You need your saber! At least I'm not afraid of a mouse. And I'm not so vain as to smear boot blacking on my whiskers."

"Vain, am I?" flung back Councillor De Groot. "You're a fine one to talk! A gullible idiot!"

And at that, the three worthies began squabbling among themselves more hotly than they had complained about their portrait.

"Gentlemen, a little more dignity!" put in Hillesum. "Or you'll have me believe I did too well by you. You wanted to be shown wise, brave, and handsome? What can be wiser than a cat who knows his way in the world? Or bolder than a prowling tom? Or handsomer than a well-groomed house cat? In any case, no cat would be so foolish as to pretend being other than he is. Alas, I fear I paid you too great a compliment."

Hearing this, the councillors left off quarreling and glanced sheepishly at one another; until, finally, Vorwick began chuckling and goodnaturedly clapped his colleagues on the back. "Come along, Trumble, you're not the first wise man who ever made a fool of himself."

"I can't blame you for being frightened of a mouse," replied Trumble. "To tell the truth, they unnerve me, too."

"The cat is right," admitted De Groot. "That orange-and-white fellow does have a certain flair. I wish I had as much."

And so they agreed that Hillesum had indeed painted them better than they deserved; and they paid every guilder they had promised. By this time, like a true artist, Master Van Eck had concluded that the only reasonable thing to do in the midst of disaster was to get up and eat breakfast; and when he learned how well Hillesum had done, in gratitude he insisted the cat be the one to sign the canvas.

As for the councillors, they decided their best gift would be not only new cobblestones, but a pleasure garden and a company of uniformed night watchmen; with horse trough, bell, and clock added for good measure. The portrait, however, they kept and hung in their council chamber to remind themselves: better cats than jackasses.

The Cat and the Fiddler

THERE WAS ONCE a young street fiddler named Nicholas. Though a good musician, he earned only the slimmest living; indeed, so poor he was that he could not even afford to keep a cat. One night, when he was in bed, he heard a tapping at his door. "Now, who can that be?" he asked himself. "Stock, the merchant, or Groschen, the banker, begging me to write a serenade for one of their grand affairs? Better yet, the King himself inviting me to play at court? Well, if it's good news it will keep; if bad, it can wait."

So he pulled the quilt over his head; but the tapping went on until at last he had to get up and unlatch the door. There on the threshold he saw a black cat with white paws and a white star on his forehead.

"You're worse off than I am if you haven't a bed to sleep in or a roof above your head," said Nicholas. "Come in, friend, for it's a cool night to be roaming the streets."

The cat graciously thanked him and at the fiddler's invitation sat down on a stool. Nicholas had been saving a cup of milk and a heel of bread for his meal next day; nevertheless, he offered it to the cat, who replied:

"It's rare enough, Master Nicholas, to find someone who'd give up his food to a human stranger, let alone to a cat. But no, thank you, I'm not hungry."

"Lucky cat," said Nicholas. "Curl up at the fireplace, then. I'm sorry there's no fire in it; even so, you're welcome to stay."

Again, the cat refused, saying:

"That's very kind of you, but the favor I came to ask is something other. Tonight, we cats hold our weekly ball. Our fiddler has gone traveling and we urgently need someone to play for us. Will you oblige?"

"That's the best offer I've had all week," said Nicholas. "In fact, the only one. You cats must have better ears for music than most of the townsfolk. Yes, I'll do it gladly."

When the cat asked what his fee would be, Nicholas only laughed and said:

"If it were Merchant Stock or Banker Groschen, I'd know how to set a price. But—fiddling for cats? Let it be a gift. My pleasure will be fee enough."

"In that case," the cat said, "be so good as to follow me."

Nicholas put on his clothes, took up his fiddle and bow, and went outside with the cat. In the street, he saw waiting a splendid coach drawn by a fine pair of white horses. The coachman was a striped cat in gold livery, on his head a cocked hat with a red rosette. The postilion, another cat also handsomely garbed, sprang down to open the door.

"I must say," Nicholas remarked, settling himself beside his companion, "when you cats do something, you do it in style."

"Naturally," said the cat. "What did you expect?"

The coach set off briskly and Nicholas leaned back to enjoy the unforeseen luxury. As the curtains were closely buckled, he could see nothing beyond them and had no idea in the world where he was being taken. The cat, meanwhile, had opened a leather case from which he took an excellently tailored jacket, a pair of kidskin gloves, and gleaming black boots. These he pulled on, as well as a silken sash with a gold-hilted sword; and set a plumed hat on his head.

"We cats are usually content to go about our business in everyday fur," he said. "On special occasions, however, it pleases us to show a little more flair. As Master of Revels, I feel I should set a certain tone."

The coach halted, its passengers descended, and Nicholas found himself in a part of town he could no way recognize. So, he had to follow the cat, who led him down a flight of stone steps to an oaken door. There, his guide knocked softly in a special way. A slate-gray cat, wearing a silver chain, opened at the signal, bowed deeply, and gestured for the new arrivals to enter.

Inside, Nicholas was so bedazzled at first he could hardly see. Candles blazed in glittering crystal chandeliers; the polished floor shone like a mirror; the ballroom was hung with draperies of crimson velvet. Everywhere he looked were cats, more than he could count, all in their finery. Some played cards at a table covered in green baize; others chatted among themselves, or took refreshment at a sideboard laden with more kinds of delicacies than ever Nicholas had seen in his life.

After a few moments, he recognized the baker's striped tom in gallant conversation with the grocer's orange tabby, who flirtatiously tapped her admirer on the nose with her ivory fan. He saw, too, the fishmonger's cat, the hatter's cat, the corn merchant's piebald, and the cabinetmaker's tortoiseshell, all of whom greeted him with utmost cordiality.

And, in fact, when the Master of Revels announced that Nicholas had consented to fiddle for them, the whole company cheered and gave him so hearty a welcome that Nicholas was sure these cats made a happier audience than their masters and mistresses.

This put him in such high spirits that he tucked his instrument under his chin and fiddled merrily away. He fiddled out polkas and waltzes, gavottes and minuets, quadrilles and contredanses; and the delighted guests would have kept him playing without cease. Nicholas, enjoying the ball as much as the dancers, would gladly have done so. However, as the candles began guttering, the Master of Revels came to Nicholas and thanked him formally on behalf of the company.

"We have enjoyed your excellent music," said the cat, "and all urge me to make this request: Will you come back a week from tomorrow night, and play for us again?"

"Indeed I will," replied Nicholas. "You have my word on it."

The cat then handed Nicholas a little packet and led him out to the waiting coach. This time he did not accompany the fiddler, but instructed the coachman to drive him swiftly home; and, reminding Nicholas of his promise, thanked him again and wished him a good night.

It was dawn by the time Nicholas was back in his bed

chamber; and he would have sworn he had dreamed all the night's happenings had it not been for the packet in his hand. This packet he now untied and found in it four new fiddle strings, the finest he had seen, for they appeared to be spun from threads of gold.

Delighted, he immediately strung them in place of his old ones, which he had altogether worn out during his night of fiddling. When he played on them to test them, he grew all the more delighted; for they were true-tempered, in every way perfect, with a clear and beautiful tone, far better than any strings he had ever owned.

That day, as usual, he went out into the town and chose what he hoped would be a likely street corner, where he struck up a lively tune to draw the passers. Still elated by the cat's gift, he paid no mind to anyone who might drop a coin into his cap. Instead, he fiddled away more for his own pleasure than otherwise.

He had scarcely begun when Merchant Stock came by. Customarily, this grand personage turned a deaf ear to the fiddler's music and had never thrown so much as a penny into the fiddler's cap. But this time the merchant halted in front of Nicholas and, staring down his nose at him, declared:

"Fiddler, I require your services. You will compose a serenade for my garden party. It must be the best quality, all new, nothing secondhand, and no warmed-over tunes that everyone has heard before. You yourself will play it. And, mind you, no skimping on the notes. I want plenty of them for my money."

And Merchant Stock named a handsome fee, more than Nicholas could hope to earn in half a year.

"Gladly!" cried Nicholas. "You'll have the finest serenade in the world! And my new fiddle strings will make it all the better!"

"Have it ready without fail, then," warned Stock, "and come to my house a week from tonight."

"A week from tonight?" returned Nicholas, dismayed. "Sir, that's not possible. I have another engagement exactly then."

"An engagement? You?" retorted the merchant. "Oho, I see the game. Yes, you musicians are all rascals and you want more money. Well, I have neither time nor inclination to dicker. So, double the sum, and that's my last offer."

"Alas, alas," cried Nicholas, "I've already promised myself elsewhere. But if you could only give your party a night later, or sooner, or any other time whatever—"

"Out of the question," snapped the merchant. "My plans are set, I've no mind to change them. All the town gentry have accepted my invitation. You could not possibly have an engagement more important than my garden party."

"Sir, I've given my word," replied Nicholas. "I'm to play for the cats' ball."

"What?" shouted Stock. "Are you serious? I never heard of such a thing! Fiddle for a pack of alley rabbits? You prefer them to me and my guests? How dare you! Go to the devil, then, you miserable scraper! You'll never again have business from me!"

Fuming, the merchant stamped off, leaving Nicholas to regret losing such a fat fee. However, Nicholas finally shrugged and told himself: Since he never had it to begin with, he could hardly miss it. In addition to keeping his word, he decided that indeed he would rather play for the town cats than for Merchant Stock. So, more than ever, he looked forward to the end of the week.

When that evening came, Nicholas impatiently waited in his chamber. No sooner had the town clock finished striking midnight than he heard a tapping at his door. It was the cat come to fetch him and, as before, the coach carried him to the ball, where the company welcomed him with still greater warmth. He played even better than the first time; and when the dancing ended, the elegant Master of Revels thanked him ceremoniously, adding:

"Your music has given us the greatest pleasure. Will you come back, tomorrow night a week, and play for us again?"

"Gladly," replied Nicholas. "So I promised you, and so I will."

The cat then handed him a long, slender packet and, reminding him of their engagement, thanked him once more and wished him a good night. At home, Nicholas untied the packet and found therein the handsomest fiddlestick he had ever seen; so lithe and light that when he drew it across the strings it seemed he was playing with a sunbeam.

That day on the street corner, Nicholas fiddled away so happily that he was at first unaware of Banker Groschen, who had come up to him and was shouting into his ear:

"Leave off! I have important business in hand. Two Court Councillors, a Minister of State, and every high official in the town will attend my next banquet. I hire you to provide music for their entertainment." And he named a sum even larger than the merchant's.

Nicholas heard this with delight, but his face fell as the banker went on:

"Come to my house a week from tonight. Fail me in this, you rogue, and I'll never deal with you again."

"Dear sir, any time but then!" cried Nicholas. "That very night I've given my word to play at the cats' ball."

At this, Groschen's face went crimson and he burst out:

"What nonsense is that? Unheard of! Do you put miauling guttersnipes ahead of my banquet guests? Ingrate! Arrogant whelp!"

Groschen's furious upbraiding had drawn a crowd of onlookers, and the banker now turned to them:

"Did you hear this idiot? He tells me he'd rather fiddle for cats than councillors! The fellow's not only disrespectful, he's witless into the bargain!"

The onlookers began hooting and guffawing at the protesting Nicholas, miauling like cats, and tapping their forefingers on their temples. Still raging, Banker Groschen strode away, leaving Nicholas bemused at himself for having turned down two fortunes in as many weeks.

Nevertheless, his new strings and his new fiddlestick cheered him; and, at the end of the week, when the coach arrived, he was in the best of spirits. He played for the dancing cats with such liveliness and grace that the Master of Revels could hardly express his gratitude.

"Surely, you won't refuse to join us next week," said the cat. "Meet us here again, give us your word on it."

"That I will," declared Nicholas, "and never fail."

Home again, he untied the package the cat had given him as usual on his departure. Inside was the most beautiful fiddle he had ever seen. Instantly he set about playing it, and found its voice as magnificent as its appearance. So joyful he was that he kicked up his heels and went laughing and dancing around his chamber. In the morning, without having bothered sleeping, he skipped through town to his corner, so entranced by the cat's gift he did not notice a splendid carriage halt in front of him.

"You there!" called the occupant. "Come here at once. I must have words with you."

When Nicholas saw who addressed him, his bow slipped and his jaw slackened; for it was the Lord Chamberlain of the Realm.

"Stop gaping and listen to me carefully," the dignitary ordered. "His Majesty commands you to play at court. It is beneath the dignity of royalty to discuss the crass matter of a fee; but you will, I assure you, be more than generously rewarded."

Nicholas could hardly believe his ears. But what he thought was good fortune soured into disaster as the Lord Chamberlain named the very day Nicholas had promised the cats. When the despairing Nicholas explained his predicament and begged to be summoned any other time, the official gave him an icy stare, and said:

"His Majesty will hear no excuse, least of all concerning cats. Furthermore, you have no choice. This is a Royal Command. Dare to refuse and you shall be punished for insubordination, low treason, high treason, and mutinous conspiracy."

The Lord Chamberlain drove off without another word, leaving Nicholas pleading and protesting, quaking in his boots, clearly seeing himself thrown into the royal dungeons, hanged, drawn, and quartered; and even having his fiddle confiscated.

For the rest of the week, the poor fellow expected a regiment of the King's Grenadiers to arrive one moment to the next and haul him away to block, scaffold, or cell. Nevertheless, he had given his promise and could only keep it. On the day of the cats' ball, he left his corner earlier than usual and bolted himself into his chamber.

Well before midnight, he heard a tapping at his door. Thinking it must be the cat arriving ahead of time, he hurried to draw the bolt. But, instead of the Master of Revels, it was none other than the King himself.

"Your Majesty!" stammered the terrified Nicholas. "Has Your Majesty come in person to chop off my head? Spare yourself the labor! Sire, believe me, I meant you no offense."

"I have no intention of chopping off your head," replied the King. "I have enough competent individuals to perform such a task. You must understand that I commanded you to play at court not for my entertainment, but for my daughter's. We have fiddlers by the dozens and, as far as I am concerned, one is as bad as the next. However, the Princess desires to hear you and no other. She insists on it absolutely. So, as a father, not a king, I am here to entreat you to go with me to the palace. I am told you have a previous appointment. But oblige me in this and you will have ample time to keep your other pressing engagement."

As the King was willing to accommodate himself to the fiddler's situation, Nicholas could do no less than accommodate himself to the King's. So he agreed and the King conducted him to the royal coach waiting at the door.

"The Princess, alas, is much given to whims and fancies," the King said, as they set out for the palace. "And now she has taken this latest notion, and Baron Sternbraue encourages her in it. For all I know, he might well have put the idea into her head in the first place. The Baron has more influence with her than I, or the whole court, for that matter.

"She does nothing without consulting him," the King went on gloomily. "Now it is time for her to marry, but she will only choose a husband of whom Baron Sternbraue approves. Suitors have come from every noble house in the kingdom. At the Baron's urging, she has turned each of them away. Most of them being nincompoops, in this case I commend the Baron's taste and judgment. But the question still goes unsettled and my daughter still unwed."

And the King fell to sighing heavily as any father with a difficult daughter, so complaining of Baron Sternbraue that Nicholas himself began dreading the power of this redoubtable courtier.

The coach by now had reached the palace, where the King himself escorted Nicholas down marble corridors lined with ranks of saluting guards and bowing footmen. The Grand Reception Hall was crowded with attendants, courtiers, and high officers of state. The bewildered Nicholas recognized the Lord Chamberlain, but wondered which, among so many dignitaries, could be the formidable Baron Sternbraue.

However, he gave up all such speculation the instant he saw the Princess, who observed his approach from her satin-cushioned chair of state. To Nicholas, she was the most beautiful and brightest young woman he had ever set eyes upon. And, while he did not fall in love with her exactly at first sight, he did so in less time than it took him to tune his fiddle strings; and if he rightly judged the light in her own eyes, the Princess was far from being ill-disposed toward him.

But when the Princess requested him to play, his heart began fluttering, his head spinning, his knees quaking; and his fingers trembling so violently they fumbled up and down the strings; his bow scraped and skittered; and, indeed, he nearly dropped his fiddle to the floor. The King rolled his eyes in dismay, the courtiers snickered and looked askance at one another. But the Princess, gazing straight at the despairing Nicholas, declared:

"You are the one I choose to wed."

"Dearest Princess!" cried Nicholas, as jubilant now as he had been distressed before. "I played badly when I meant to play my best. Even so, how glad I am that my fiddling has won your heart!"

"Most certainly it has not," the Princess frankly replied, fondly smiling nevertheless. "I've never in all my life heard such abominable scraping and scratching. Yes, you have won my heart. But I confess you did so even before you set bow to strings. However, I will not marry—"

"Good heavens, girl, what are you saying?" broke in the King. "First you'll wed, then you won't? If you love each other, what's a sour-note or two? Let him take a few lessons, he's bound to improve."

The Princess raised her hand and went on:

"I will not marry without the approval of Baron Sternbraue."

Nicholas groaned to himself, shaking with fear at the prospect of being judged by the all-powerful nobleman. He waited, breathless, as the Princess called for the Baron to come forward and give his opinion.

From behind her chair stepped a black cat with white paws and a white star on his forehead.

"You? Is it you?" stammered Nicholas. "You, the Master of Revels? And you, Baron Sternbraue?"

"One and the same," replied the cat. "Generally speaking, we cats put no store in rank or titles. However, since it amuses the Princess to call me thus, in this case I don't object to it."

The cat then turned and said to the Princess:

"This young man offered me shelter and his last morsel of food without even knowing who I was. He kept his word, though keeping it might have cost him his head. He has shown himself kindhearted, steadfast, and true—which is more than can be said of your noble suitors; or, indeed, of most fiddlers. Your Grace, you have my full approval."

The courtiers applauded, the King wept tears of joy; but just as Nicholas and the Princess were about to

110

throw their arms around each other, the clock began striking midnight.

"Fiddler," said the cat, "I believe you have an engagement elsewhere."

Nicholas clapped a hand to his head. "So I do. Princess, excuse me. You understand—"

"Never fret," put in the cat. "Tonight, the Princess shall go with you."

Leaving King and courtiers to celebrate without them, Nicholas and the Princess followed the cat to the palace gate. From there, the waiting coach sped them to the ball. When Baron Sternbraue announced the joyful news, the company cheered the loving pair to the echo. Since the cats' own fiddler had returned from his travels, it was he who now played for the guests, while Nicholas and the Princess danced together until dawn.

And so they were married. Though Nicholas would have been proud to be known simply as the dear husband of the Princess, the King named him First Fiddler of the Realm. Despite this imposing title, whenever he was invited to play at the cats' ball, Nicholas was delighted to accept.

And, since the Princess and Nicholas followed their cat's advice in all important matters, of course they lived happily ever after.

The Apprentice Cat

In the village of Holgerborg lived Master Bushelby
and his good wife Berta. They had no children, but kept
a young striped cat named Witling. Despite their slender
circumstances, they never skimped on his care and comfort. They brushed him, combed him, scrubbed his ears,
and polished his whiskers; and saved him all choice
morsels from their frugal meals. Fond of the couple as
they were of him, Witling happily passed his kittenhood
in their tidy cottage. But one day Master Bushelby spoke
aside with his wife:

"Our Witling is a fine cat," he said, "and we must help
him make his way in the world. The time has come for
him to learn a trade."

"So it has," agreed Mistress Berta. "But which trade
should he follow?"

And so they considered one occupation after the
other, and whether Witling should be a blacksmith, or
stonecutter, or a carpenter; a tailor, a cabinetmaker, or
a cobbler. But none seemed fitting. At last, Mistress
Berta said:

"Such tender paws our Witling has, they're soft as
velvet gloves. What better for milking cows? And you

know he's very partial to a drop of cream and a bit of cheese. Would he not make a fine dairyman?"

"A most excellent one," declared Bushelby. "And so shall he be."

They called Witling to them and told him what had been decided: that he would be apprentice to Master Curdle, the dairy farmer.

"We want you to be successful in your life," said Bushelby, "and prosperous in your occupation."

"We want you to be happy," added Mistress Berta, "and to make us proud of you."

Witling, by disposition, was a merry-hearted, easy-natured cat; and at the same time, a well-meaning one. Never until now had he given a moment's thought to being successful and prosperous. However, seeing the grave faces of his master and mistress, he understood it must indeed be an important matter. So he dutifully answered:

"What a lucky cat I am to have such good things in store. If dairying's to be my trade, you can be sure I'll do my best at it."

All being arranged, Witling was taken to Master Curdle's dairy, there to serve his apprenticeship. The first morning Witling was gone from the cottage, Mistress Berta wept into her apron. Her husband, looking gray and solemn, went about tugging his side-whiskers and sighing through his nose. Nevertheless, they consoled and assured each other they had done the proper thing.

For his part, much as he missed his kindly guardians and snug little home, Witling was delighted in his apprenticeship. He sniffed the fragrant hay in the milk-

115

ing shed; his eyes brightened at the thought of sporting with the mice in the straw; the lowing of the cows soothed his ears. There were pannikins of delicious clotted cream, tubs of butter, wheels of ripe cheese a-plenty, and he told himself:

"This dairy trade must be the pleasantest in the world. How clever of my master and mistress to choose it for me."

He began scampering through the straw, rolling on his back, clambering in and out of the mangers, and swinging from the tails of the astonished cows. But Master Curdle, a bull-necked fellow with bands of muscles across his shoulders, and arms thick as sides of beef, told him sternly:

"Now, then, young Witling, none of that. You're here to learn your work and earn your keep."

And he set Witling to raking out the stalls, and sweeping and scrubbing, fetching and carrying. Then he put him at the butter churn; and Witling was obliged to plunge the dasher up and down, up and down, till his whiskers drooped and he was weary from the end of his nose to the tip of his tail.

"What kind of trade is this?" groaned Witling. "There's more blisters than butter to it!"

The churning done, Curdle tied a white apron around Witling's middle, sat his apprentice on a three-legged stool, and showed him how to milk, warning him that he must fill all the pails before midday.

Though dismayed at how much labor lay ahead of him, Witling reminded himself that his master and mistress wanted the best for him, that he was to be

116

prosperous and make them proud; and he pumped away in all good earnest. But after a time, his mouth grew so dry and his throat so parched he could barely swallow. The milk smelled so sweet and looked so inviting, with the rich cream foaming on top, that he had to have a taste of it. He climbed from the stool, put his paws on the rim of the pail, and thrust in his head. At first, he only dipped in the tip of his tongue; but one sip led to another, and soon he was lapping joyfully.

Master Curdle, that moment, came into the shed. At sight of Witling drinking cream to his heart's content, the dairyman shook the broom he was carrying and bellowed at the cat:

"Leave off! Greedy beast, you're guzzling up all my profit!"

Startled by Curdle's outbursts, Witling tumbled head-first into the pail, which overturned with a clatter, spilling out both cat and cream. This, in turn, alarmed the cow, who kicked up her heels, broke loose from the stall, and so terrified her neighbors that they all dashed bawling from the shed.

Choking and sputtering, fur sopping with milk, Witling streaked through the dairy with Curdle in hot pursuit. Springing to the high mounds of cheese, Witling set them spinning and rolling like so many millstones. Jumping clear, he upset the churn, knocked over the tub of butter; and by the time Curdle was able to catch him, the dairy was a shambles.

"See what you've done!" roared the dairyman. "Worthless cat! Good for nothing!"

Seizing Witling by the scruff of the neck, Master

Curdle never stopped upbraiding him until he had brought him back to the Bushelbys' cottage and left him there, vowing to have the law on them if ever again he laid eyes on that cat.

Dismayed though they were, the good couple did not reproach Witling. They dried his fur, brushed him until he glistened, soothed and stroked him until the unhappy Witling was quite himself again.

"The fault is ours, not our Witling's," Master Bushelby told his wife. "The dairy trade hardly suits him as well as we had supposed."

"Our Witling's no way cut out to be a dairyman," said Mistress Berta. "But, then, whatever shall he be?"

"You know how quick and clever our Witling is," replied Bushelby, after several moments, "how sharp his eyes, and how deft he is at catching a strand of your yarn. Now that I think it over: What better trade for him than weaving?"

"Weaving!" exclaimed Mistress Berta. "Why, of course! The very thing! What a marvelous idea!"

Bushelby nodded sagely. "Merely a question of understanding one's natural proclivities. Then, all comes right."

And so Witling was taken as apprentice to Master Heddle, the weaver, a dry, dour little man whose lank hair dangled in a ragged fringe. After what had happened to him in the dairy, Witling was at first wary of this new apprenticeship. But the weaving room, with its neatly ranged shelves of yarn, pots of dye, and bolts of finished cloth, was bright and sunny, and never a speck of dust on the polished floor.

"It seems a clean, comfortable line of business,"

thought Witling. "If only I'd been sent here in the first place. At least, I've learned one good lesson: Never drink milk on the job."

And so, when Heddle set him on the weaving bench to teach him how to work the loom, Witling watched and listened closely, polite and respectful as ever Master Bushelby and Mistress Berta could wish.

However, as the shuttle darted back and forth like a mouse among the threads, Witling's eyes began to glint. His haunches wriggled, his tail lashed back and forth, and his paws itched after the fascinating object; until at last unable to resist such a tempting lure, Witling leaped from the bench and plunged into the maze of threads. Yowling heroically, he pounced on the elusive shuttle, kicking gaily with his hind legs, and tangling himself in the loom like a fly in a spider web.

Squealing with rage as threads broke left and right, Master Heddle strove to pull Witling loose; but the weaver's frantic efforts only toppled the loom and sent the frame crashing to the floor.

"Get out of that! Let go, you idiot cat!" Heddle cried, as warp and weft unraveled in a twinkling. "There's all my work undone!"

Witling had just been thinking that weaving must be the merriest trade of all; but, hearing Master Heddle's furious yells and glimpsing the weaver's face, with all speed he scrambled from the tangled threads and raced for the safety of the highest shelves. The weaver set off nimbly after him; however, by the time Master Heddle was able to lay hands on Witling, the skeins of yarn and bolts of cloth had all gone flying. The dye pots upset, spattering both weaver and apprentice with every color of the rainbow.

Snatching up Witling and holding the dripping cat at arm's length, the weaver hustled his would-be apprentice to the Bushelbys, shook his fist, and swore to send them a bill for damages. Shamefaced, Witling hid in the corner; and so bedaubed he was with spots and streaks of orange, blue, green, and purple, the Bushelbys could scarcely recognize their little striped cat under the motley hues.

"We must blame ourselves, not our Witling," said Master Bushelby, sighing heavily. "Weaving's no more his trade than dairying. We shall have to find another occupation that better suits his talents."

"Husband," replied Mistress Berta, "I know what it is. Have you ever seen our Witling when he drowses on your lap, how happily his little claws go in and out, in and out, as if the dear creature was kneading dough for bread? Baking's the trade he should follow."

"Baking?" exclaimed Bushelby. "Indeed so! How did we not think of that before? Our Witling's a born baker if ever there was one!"

Having cleaned the spots and streaks from Witling's fur and whiskers, the good couple now gave him into the charge of the baker, Master Crust.

Witling, for his part, was more than ever distrustful and uneasy after the happenings at the weaver's; but Master Crust looked a jolly fellow, round and plump, with a dumpling nose and eyes shiny as two black currants.

"Never fear," declared Crust, as he clapped a tall

white hat on Witling's head. "We'll make a baker of you yet."

Then he took Witling to the kneading trough and set him to kneading the great slabs of dough, which the cat did very well indeed, just as Mistress Berta had foretold. And soon Witling began feeling altogether pleased with his new trade.

"At last," he said to himself, "here's the work for me, better than dairying and weaving. But at least I've learned two thing: to keep my nose out of milk pails and my paws away from anything that moves."

So, tempted though he was, Witling paid no mind to the basins of milk, jugs of sweet cream, and tubs of fresh butter on the mixing table; and he firmly shut his eyes to the mice scampering about the flour bins. Instead, he busily kneaded away, seeing himself a successful, prosperous baker, and thinking how proud of him the Bushelbys would be.

Next, Master Crust showed Witling how to shape the dough into loaves and, with a long wooden bread shovel, slide them into the oven.

"They must bake neither too long nor too short," said Crust, "neither overdone nor underdone, but just right. So, keep good watch and call me when they're nice and golden."

Assuring the baker he would not stir so much as a hair from the spot, Witling sat down beside the oven. "This baking trade," he told himself, "gets better and better, if all I need do is sit here and let the oven do the work."

At first, Witling sat bolt upright, watchful as a sentry at his guard box. Soon, however, the warmth from the oven made his eyelids heavy, and he began yawning drowsily. Since he had steadfastly kept from lapping milk and chasing mice, he saw no harm in catching forty winks. So, finally, he lay down on the brick floor, curled his tail around him, tucked his paws under his chin, and soon was happily purring away, cozy and content, as if napping by his own cottage hearth.

But after a while, a sharp odor made his nostrils twitch. He coughed and sneezed himself awake. Blinking open his eyes, which immediately began watering and smarting, Witling jumped to his feet. Clouds of smoke poured from the oven. Yelling for Master Crust, Witling pulled open the oven door, blistering his paws and singeing his whiskers. Inside, the whole day's baking lay not golden brown but cinder black, and burning briskly as matchwood.

Snatching up the basin of milk, Witling dashed it into the flames; he flung in the cream jug, pelted the fire with eggs, and smothered it with flour. By this time, the breathless baker had come running; but instead of commending the cat for putting out the fire, Master Crust stamped his feet and tore at his hair. His pudgy face crumbled like a stale buscuit, and his jolly disposition went up in smoke along with the rest of his wares.

"My loaves!" wailed the baker. "My beautiful bread! You lazy beast! You ne'er-do-well!"

Before Witling could escape, Master Crust seized him by the tail, tossed him into an empty flour sack, and hauled him back to the Bushelbys' cottage. "If that worthless cat ever sets foot in my shop," he roared, "I swear I'll bake him into a pie!"

If Mistress Berta had wept the first time Witling left the cottage, she wept twice as hard now to see him come back in such a state; and Master Bushelby sighed, groaned, and rolled his eyes in dismay.

"We have ourselves to blame, not our Witling," said Mistress Berta, as she and her husband scraped away Witling's coat of flour. "He's not meant to be a baker, no more than a dairyman nor weaver."

To comfort the disconsolate Witling, Mistress Berta poured a little milk into a saucer and put it down by the fireplace, then sat herself in a chair across from her husband; and the two of them tried once again to think of a proper trade for their unfortunate cat.

"Do you suppose," Master Bushelby said, after a time, "that he might do well as a sailor?"

"Good heavens, no!" replied Mistress Berta. "Go off to sea? And get himself all tattooed? Only think how long he'd be away from us before his ship came back to port. And the storms and the waves! Why, the poor thing would be terrified. He's better off at home," she went on. "Just look at him now. How happy he is, drinking his saucer of milk."

"So he is," agreed Master Bushelby. "And see how neatly he does it with his little pink tongue, never spilling a drop. I'd never noticed before what a fine milk drinker our Witling is."

"Yes, and he does enjoy a piece of broiled herring, too," said Mistress Berta. "What if he studied to be a fishmonger?"

"An honest calling, but a rather odoriferous one," replied Master Bushelby. "Perhaps, instead, he should go into law?"

"What, and keep company with such rascals?"

answered Mistress Berta. "It would spoil his character altogether."

Witling had been paying no heed to this conversation. The saucer of milk had put him back in fine fettle; he was more than ever glad to be home; and in such high spirits that he began scampering after Mistress Berta's ball of yarn, tossing it into the air, seizing it between his paws, and turning one somersault after another.

Observing these antics, Master Bushelby spoke up again:

"It occurs to me that he could be a splendid acrobat. He's quick on his feet as any I've seen at the town fair."

"Would you have him travel with a circus?" returned Mistress Berta. "With fire eaters and snake charmers, poor thing? Though now, as you mention it, I see what a fine juggler and tumbler he is, And he would look handsome in spangles."

Witling, meanwhile, had tired of his game. After such a day, he wanted nothing better than to sleep in the glow of the fireplace. So he stretched out on the hearth and purred himself into slumber.

Master Bushelby and Mistress Berta watched him fondly. Witling's happy purring so charmed and soothed them, they both sat quiet and thoughtful, smiling first at their cat, then at each other.

"Wife," said Master Bushelby at last, "I think I know the best trade of all for our Witling: a house cat."

"Husband," replied Mistress Berta, "I was about to say the same. We wanted him successful, prosperous, and happy. And so he is, exactly as he should be."

With that, the good couple decided the finest thing in

the world for Witling was indeed to let him be what he had always been; and they were proud to have him follow an occupation for which he was truly suited.

As for Witling, no matter how he had served his other apprenticeships, he was a master at being a cat; which, in itself, was already a quite remarkable achievement.

MS READ-a-thon—
a simple way to start youngsters reading

Boys and girls between 6 and 14 can join the MS READ-a-thon and help find a cure for Multiple Sclerosis by reading books. And they get two rewards—the enjoyment of reading, and the great feeling that comes from helping others.

Parents and educators: For complete information call your local MS chapter. Or mail the coupon below.

Kids can help, too!

Mail to:
National Multiple Sclerosis Society
205 East 42nd Street
New York, N.Y. 10017
I would like more information about the MS READ-a-thon and how it can work in my area.

MS Mystery Sleuth™

Name _____
(please print)
Address _____
City _____ State _____ Zip _____
Organization _____

1—81